SECOND CHANCE AT LOVE

An LUW Romance Anthology

Second Chance at Love
An LUW Romance Anthology

Copyright © 2022 by the LUW Romance Chapter

Individual works are Copyright © 2022 by their respective authors.

All rights reserved. The stories in this book are the property of their respective authors, in all media both physical and digital. No one, except the owners of this property, may reproduce, copy, or publish in any medium any individual story or part of this anthology without the express permission of the author of the work.

The contents of this book are fiction. Any resemblance to any actual person, place, or event is purely coincidental. Any opinions expressed by the authors are their own and do not reflect those of the editors or League of Utah Romance Chapter.

Cover design © 2022 by League of Utah Romance Chapter
Cover designed by Austin Slade Perry
Edited by Elizabeth Suggs, Jonathan Reddoch, and Talysa Sainz

Contents

Introduction

The League of Utah Writers Romance Chapter, a nonprofit writing group, is proud to present our very first printed book, *Second Chance*, an LUW Romance Anthology. The theme was originally inspired by reunited lovers, but quickly expanded into something more—the possibility to give love a second chance, even if that love was from someone new.

Second Chance brings together a vast assortment of highly talented writers who write in romance or use romance in their writing. In this anthology, we've got a gay ballet romp, a rendezvous with a ghost, an erotic love story (don't worry, our erotic stories have content warnings), and even a first date fiasco— that's just four of ten amazing stories, each with their own unique style.

So, whether you are a diehard romantic reader or this is your first time chance with romance, you've picked up a wonderful collection. You won't be disappointed.

And once you've read our book, please show your appreciation by reviewing us on Goodreads and Amazon. Reviews help others see the greatness of our writers and keep us publishing more anthologies.

Elizabeth Suggs
President of the LUW Romance Chapter
Owner of Editing Mee
Co-owner of Collective Tales Publishing

Weekend in the Woods

Stacy Wrytes

Logan turned the key and opened the door to Dad's old fishing cabin. The creak of the hinges reminded him of father-son trips and standing side-by-side trying to fix the did-it-themselves wiring or the forever-leaking plumbing. It had been two years since his father had passed away and a few more since Logan had come to the cabin, but stepping through the door was like stepping back in time.

Back to a better time.

Don't think about it, Logan, he told himself and rubbed at the ache in his chest. He wouldn't let the pain swallow him up anymore. Dad was gone. He missed him every day. But every day, it got a little easier to breathe.

Logan dropped his backpack next to the ancient couch that sagged in the middle. He walked past the table with the one leg that they'd never gotten around to fixing and entered the tiny galley kitchen. Everything was clean but for the slightest coating of dust. Jake Davis did a great job keeping the cabin in livable shape, even if it was rarely used. But he was getting older and wanted to move closer to his daughter, which meant Logan couldn't avoid it any longer. It was time to let the cabin go.

His father had wanted to donate the land and the cabin to the Forest Service after his death, but Logan had put off the transfer. He'd used the excuse that Morgan, his sister, frequently visited the cabin. But after taking a teaching job in a remote location, she confessed she wouldn't have time for weekend trips to the cabin anymore.

The sound of vehicles and then doors opening and closing drew Logan's attention.

"The septic tank is in good shape, and the cabin runs on solar," a man's voice said. "But I'll need to light the pilot light for the water heater." *Jake?* Logan recognized the caretaker's voice, but who was he speaking to?

"Are you sure no one's here?" a different and decidedly female voice asked. "There's a car parked outside." There was something achingly familiar about the voice.

Logan started toward the door.

"There's a small trail behind the cabin," Jake explained. "I'm sure they just wanted to park closer than the public lot on the other side of the lake." The door knob jiggled and the front door opened. "But I can wait around if you're worried about them bothering you."

"No, I'm sure you're right." She stepped into the cabin. "I'll be fine..."

Logan's gaze connected with Hannah Summers as her voice trailed off. He couldn't look away. She hadn't changed in the past two years. Although, the last time he'd seen her she'd been wearing scrubs. Today, she had on a pair of shorts that showed off her long, toned legs, and a plaid shirt knotted at her waist, revealing a figure that scrubs had always concealed but that Logan had suspected was there.

Then the memories of their last encounter caught up to him, and the heat building inside him cooled. Logan hadn't taken the news of his father's death well. To say he'd "shot the messenger" would be a monumental understatement. He'd nearly thrown Hannah out of the house and accused her of murder.

What was she doing here?

Jake peeked around the side of the door. "Oh, Logan, I didn't know you'd be here."

Logan pulled his gaze from Hannah. "Hey, Jake, I'm sorry I didn't tell you. I wasn't aware the cabin was going to be in use."

"I'm so sorry, Mr. Casey." Hannah's movements were stiff and awkward, like she didn't want to be near him. "Morgan said the cabin was available this weekend."

Unlike him, Morgan had stayed friends with Hannah after their father's death. She hadn't blamed the hospice nurse for their father's inevitable passing. For years he'd told himself Morgan had smoothed over any hurt he'd caused, but Hannah's caution and formality said otherwise.

"I'm sorry," she looked back at her car. "I'll just..."

"No, it's fine." Logan held up his hand to stop her. "It's my fault. I didn't tell Morgan I was coming here." He turned his gaze to Jake. "And I should've checked with you too, Jake. I apologize."

"It's your place, so I don't see a reason to apologize to me." Jake rubbed his hand over his jet-black hair. "But it does leave us with a bit of a situation. There aren't many other places to stay on the lake."

"It's fine." Hannah straightened her spine. "I'll just head home. I really didn't need a weekend in the woods." She rushed out the door.

"Wait a second." Before Logan realized what he was doing, he was following after her.

"So, I'll just uhh… I'll just get the water heater working," Jake said and disappeared into the house leaving Logan to pursue the fleeing nurse.

3

* * *

"Hannah, wait!" Logan called from the porch.

Her name on his lips brought Hannah to a stop and flooded her mind with bittersweet memories of late-night board games, bedside conversations, and one gentle goodnight kiss. She hadn't been able to forget the way he looked at her or the way it made her feel.

"Hannah, wait, I'm the one that should leave." He stopped behind her. "Morgan offered the cabin to you. I should've checked before coming up. After all, she uses it more than I do."

She turned to face him. "But that's even more reason for you to stay."

When he'd appeared in the doorway, she'd been too shocked to really look at him. Here in the early evening sun, she gave herself permission to study him. She'd seen pictures of him, of course. Morgan posted pictures on social media.

Hannah had watched the man she'd spent three months getting closer than was professionally advisable, turn into a stranger. The laughter in his eyes was replaced with sadness. His healthy fit body became alarmingly thin. So many times she had wanted to reach out to him, but knew she was the last person he'd want to see.

Now, the person standing in front of her was healthier than the grief-stricken man she'd seen in pictures, but his eyes still didn't reflect happiness.

Logan crossed his arms over his chest. "I can't make you drive home this late. It's almost seven. The canyons get dark early, and you won't make it home until after midnight."

"I can handle a little night driving." Hannah matched his pose. Although, the winding roads and steep drop offs hadn't been her favorite part of the trip. "And besides I'm a night owl; I like being up late."

"Yeah…I remember." A new roughness in his voice sent a tingle down her spine. She met his gaze and felt her temperature rise.

"Logan, I—" She looked away. "I can't kick you out of your own cabin."

She'd made a point he couldn't argue and turned toward her car. The last thing she ever wanted to do was cause Logan more trouble. He was right about her not looking forward to the drive. She rounded the car and opened the door. The sooner she started, the sooner it would be over.

"What if…" He stood next to her car. "What if we both stayed?"

Hannah stared at him over the hood.

"We're both adults, and we're both here," he continued. "I know the cabin isn't big, but I promise to stay out of your way." He looked down at his feet. "We got along pretty good, once upon a time. And I wouldn't mind the company."

We got along? It had felt like a lot more than "getting along" to Hannah. She twisted her hands in the backpack strap on her shoulder. But those feelings were all in the past. *Weren't they?* She studied Logan's face and couldn't decipher any ulterior motives.

She took a breath and took a chance. "Okay, we'll share. Let me know if I'm in your way at all, and I'll leave." She'd been lying when she'd said she didn't need a weekend in the woods. She'd been working nonstop for the past six months and needed a recharge.

"Deal." Logan smiled. "I'll let Jake know."

She watched him head back into the cabin as butterflies materialized in her stomach. It was funny; she hadn't expected his smile to affect her that way.

* * *

The silence grew louder as the sound of Jake's truck faded and Logan wondered if he'd made a big mistake. He had the best intentions when he'd suggested they both stay, but now, the reality of the situation was settling in.

They were alone.

The moment was still vivid in his mind. Two years ago, Hannah stood in front of him in her blue scrubs with tears in her eyes. "I'm sorry, Logan. He's gone." Rather than crying, he'd lashed out, and she'd been his unfortunate target. He had destroyed any rapport between them in an instant. Even now, she avoided his gaze as she seemed to find every nook and cranny of the cabin more interesting than him.

He couldn't forget the words he'd said to her, "Don't stand there like a statue and claim you're sorry he's dead!" It still made him sick thinking about how he'd treated her. But now was his chance to make it right.

Logan cleared his throat. "So, we probably should decide on sleeping arrangements."

"Right." Hannah fiddled with the strap of her backpack. She still didn't look at him as she gazed down the small hallway. There were two bedrooms, so they wouldn't have to share. But there was definitely a better bedroom. The one on the right was bigger, had a view of the lake, with a queen-size bed that was still in good shape.

The one on the left had a few challenges. Or at least it had last time he'd used it. When he and Morgan were kids it had been fine. He'd loved looking into the forest at night. Then he'd grown too tall for the bunk beds—his feet hanging over the edge of the mattress. At that point, he started setting up a hammock out on the porch.

Unfortunately, now it was too cold for the porch, and his back was too old for a hammock. But what was most unfortunate—he was a gentleman.

"You take the one on the right." He nodded toward the better room.

"Are you sure?" She gave him a concerned look.

"Yep." He grabbed his backpack off the floor and headed for the room on the left. "You'll be able to see the lake from the window. You'll love it. Did my sister tell you to bring bedding?"

"Y-yeah, I've got sheets and blankets." She pulled her bag off her shoulder and patted the front.

"Sounds like you're all set." He turned to end the conversation, but she spoke.

"Logan." She touched his back, sending a wave of heat through him. He turned, and her hand slipped away. "I can take the bunk beds. You need a bed you can at least fit on."

She stood so close that he saw the flecks of gold in her hazel eyes, and smelled the soft coconut fragrance of her skin. It reminded him of another time, when he'd been even closer. Her soft gasp as his lips had pressed against hers. Their kiss hadn't lasted long, but it had sent a shock wave through his body, and he knew he wanted another. He pushed his heated thoughts away and shook his head. "Are we going to do this all weekend?"

"Do what?" The confusion in her gaze said she wasn't thinking about their kiss.

"Argue," he clarified. "About every little thing?"

"We're not arguing," she argued. He raised his eyebrows. "Okay, fine. I see your point."

He leaned against the wall. "So how do we solve this?"

Hannah pushed both bedroom doors open. "I'd fit better on the bunk beds. But I'll admit, it wouldn't be my first choice."

Logan smiled at her honesty. "We could always share. I'm a great cuddler."

A bark of laughter escaped before she rolled her eyes. "I forgot how you like to tease."

Only you, he didn't say aloud. But it worked—she seemed to relax. He offered another solution, "I can take the bunk beds apart and push them together. That will be almost bigger than the queen."

"Okay," she conceded. "I'll take the queen. But then I'm in charge of cooking."

Logan started to disagree, but she put her hands on her hips. "Okay, fine." He put his hands up in surrender. "Anything else we need to argue about?"

"I think I'm good—for now." Her smile could push the darkest clouds away.

"Okay." He straightened from the wall. "Go and get settled, and I'll start dismantling the bunk beds." Hannah disappeared into the nicer bedroom, and Logan turned toward the kitchen. He was pretty sure Dad's tool box was in the utility closet. And for the first time, thinking about his father didn't cause his chest to ache.

* * *

Hannah took another bite of her meal. Logan sat across from her. He hadn't said a word since they'd sat down. It seemed like the only time they could talk was when they were arguing. She knew she was a constant reminder of what he'd lost. And she didn't know how to move past it.

This was one of the dangers in getting too close to her patients and their families. She'd become too attached to the Caseys, especially to Logan. He'd been so generous, always asking if she needed something and offering to sit with his father so she could take a break. He'd taken the time to get to know her, to listen to her thoughts and feelings. He was her employer but he never treated her like she was just an employee. Was it really that surprising she'd fallen in love with him?

Hannah froze with the fork halfway to her mouth. *Love?* Where had that idea come from? Yes, she'd felt affection for him. And something had been growing between them, but love?

She glanced over at Logan. He hadn't changed from the man she'd met two years ago. He sat with his knee up to balance the wobbly leg of the table. He'd spent almost an hour dismantling the bunk beds and not once had he complained.

How had she not realized she'd fallen in love with him?

Logan raised his head and looked at her with inquiry and then confusion. Heat rose in her cheeks. "So, um," she lowered her fork, "what are your plans this weekend?"

"I plan to do a little fishing." He leaned back in his chair causing the table to wiggle slightly. "And there's some of Dad's stuff stored here I want to collect." He paused and something new colored his voice. "Really, I just wanted one more weekend before giving it up."

She looked up from her plate. "You're selling your father's cabin?"

"Donating it." He gazed around at the space. "It's what he wanted and… it's time."

Her heart clenched and an objection locked in her throat. That wasn't what his father had wanted. She was positive. "A-are you sure?"

"Yeah. I'm ready."

Then why did darkness slip into his eyes?

Hannah clenched her hands in her lap. She'd spent three months at Finn Casey's bedside. They'd spoken about everything. This cabin had been one of his favorite subjects. He'd shared countless stories of weekend trips and summers spent on the lake. When he'd mentioned his desire to give the land and cabin to the National Forest that paralleled the property, it had always souded like something for the far distant future. But what could she say? It was Logan's decision to make. She had no right to stop him.

Silence descended again. Thankfully, Logan picked up the conversation. "And what about you? What do you have planned?"

"I'm not sure." She watched him take a bite of his food. "If the weather is warm enough I'd like to go hiking."

"It might be a little chilly in the morning, but it should be nice by the afternoon. And the trails around here are well marked." He scraped together another mouthful.

"Hours of sunlight are limited so make sure you turn back well before dark. Did you bring bear spray?"

Her stomach flipped. "Bear spray…?" Morgan hadn't said anything about bears. Hannah knew bears existed in northern Washington but… she hadn't planned on encountering any.

"You okay?" Logan wiped his mouth with a napkin. "You've gone a little pale."

"I'm f-fine." She nodded. "I just hadn't planned… I didn't bring…"

"I brought a couple cans." He waved his fork. "You can borrow one."

She nodded her thanks. Maybe she would just stay near the cabin. She'd brought some novels with her. She could always read instead. Of course, reading wasn't nearly the escape she wanted. She sat at sleeping patients' beds for hours at a time; finding time to read wasn't really a struggle.

"I… I could come with you."

Hannah looked up.

"That is… if I wouldn't be in your way." His cheeks were a little pink. He cleared his throat. "I wouldn't mind you taking advantage of me in the woods."

She threw her napkin at him, and he laughed. But his teasing worked; she wasn't as nervous about hiking. "Thanks." Her face warmed. "I'd like the company."

* * *

He was a coward.

Logan followed Hannah down the hall. The longer he took to apologize the more inopportune apologizing became. He should've said something when they were first alone in the cabin, but instead he'd focused on sleeping arrangements. He had all dinner to do it too but let small talk and awkward silence fill the time. And now they were heading to bed.

He knew if he let tonight pass without saying something, he never would. But how was he supposed to start an apology that was two years too late?

She reached the door to her room and glanced over her shoulder. "Well, good night."

"Hannah." He started to reach for her but stopped. "I'm sorry."

Her head tilted slightly to one side. "For what?"

"For how I treated you." He stared at her hands to avoid her gaze. They were small but he remembered their strength when she'd touched him and their warmth when she'd pulled him close. "When my father passed. I lashed out. I said some hurtful things. I'm sorry."

Her answer was silence, and it forced him to look up.

Her expression was so gentle, his legs went weak. "Logan… you were grieving. I never once held what you said against you. I knew what you were going through."

Logan stood frozen. So many different impulses welled up inside him. He wanted to run from her compassion. He wanted to fall to his knees and let her forgiveness wash over him. He wanted to pull her into his arms and kiss her and then follow her into the room with the queen-size bed. He couldn't do all of them, so he did nothing.

"Do…" Her voice was small. "When you look at me, do you see me… or the person who told you about your father's death?" The vulnerability in her eyes made him want to hold her. "I've just always wondered."

This was his fault. He'd let his guilt make her feel this.

"No, looking at you doesn't remind me of his death." He watched a flash of relief cross her face. "Actually, seeing you… reminds me of the good times we had near the end. And I'm grateful for that."

Logan was aware of how little distance there was between them. Hannah's open expression was like a flash of déjà vu. He'd been here before, but last time was in the hallway of his father's house. Could he touch her again? Would she respond as she had before?

Instead, he stepped back. "Well, it's late."

A crooked smile touched her lips. "Yeah, it's been a long day." She turned away. "Good night, Logan."

"Good night." He watched her close the door and turned to his own room.

He really was a coward.

Logan couldn't sleep—or stop thinking about Hannah. He regretted not kissing her. There was no denying he was still drawn to her. She was the same as she'd been two years ago, but it wasn't two years ago. Things change, people change. What if she didn't remember the spark that had ignited between them? What if, for her, it had gone out?

But what if it hadn't?

He tossed and turned thinking about it. He also tossed and turned because the bunk beds hadn't worked according to plan. He lay across both beds to keep from hanging off one end, but every time he moved, the beds slid apart. At least he didn't need his alarm clock.

When morning came, he rose and left early for the lake. Hannah didn't stir while he grabbed his gear. So he left her a note saying he'd be back in time for breakfast. He fished for a few hours, catching many and throwing back most, then carried back a couple medium-sized rainbow trout to cook for lunch.

His stomach growled. Hopefully, Hannah would have breakfast ready when he arrived. But the prospect of waking her up and seeing her all rumpled also had its appeal.

Logan couldn't decide which would be better.

The smell of bacon welcomed him as he climbed the steps to the porch. He looked through the screen door and was greeted by the sight of Hannah's backside. She was under the table fiddling with the short leg. Logan took off his fishing vest and dropped his gear on the porch. The small cooler he'd brought to the lake should keep the fish for a few hours. But he honestly didn't care if they spoiled; it was amazing how quickly his priorities could

shift. He needed to write a "thank you" note to whoever
made those shorts.

* * *

The screen door squeaked and Hannah jumped, knocking her
head against the bottom of the table. "Ouch!" She pulled back.

"Hey." Logan came to her side. "Are you okay?
Sorry I startled you."

"I'm fine." She rubbed her head and looked at him.
The smile on his face was more natural and relaxed than it
had been yesterday. She hoped that meant he'd let go of his
guilt. But where did that leave them? Last night he'd looked
at her with so much passion. She'd been transported back to
that kiss and hoped they could've started up where they'd
left off. But he'd pulled away, sending her to bed, and giving her a night of restless sleep.

"I should've warned you, that leg is a lost cause."
He helped her to her feet but didn't step back, keeping her
hand in his. "Dad and I worked on this table a dozen times
and could never seem to even out the legs. He finally gave
up and said, 'If we keep cutting on it, we're going to end up
with a coffee table.'"

His laughter made her eyes well up with tears. To
see him talk about his father without an edge of pain in his
voice was worth a lump on the head. How could he let this
place go? Didn't he see how much being here was helping
him heal?

"So what's for breakfast?" He reached behind her
and grabbed a slice of bacon.

"Logan, you can't give the cabin away." His only
response was to silently chew, compelling her to continue. "I know it's not my place to say, but I don't think your
father wanted you to get rid of this place. I think he didn't
want you to feel burdened by it, so he gave you another
option." His expression gave her no clue to his thoughts,
but regardless of the outcome she cared too much to let him

walk away from something so important. "The memories of your dad… they're precious and they're here. Don't you feel closer to him in this place?"

He looked around the cabin as he seemed to consider her words. "I do have a lot of memories of Dad here. But being in this cabin can't bring him back. And I think that's okay." His gaze returned to hers, the softness there drew her in. "I don't know what I'm going to do yet. Thank you for caring, Hannah."

"Logan…" This time she reached for him. "Of course I—" Something moved over his shoulder and Hannah froze. "Bear."

* * *

It only took Logan a second to register Hannah's fear and a second more to register her words. Bear. He looked over his shoulder; a large bear had his cooler in its paw and one of his fish in its mouth. Then the sound of something tearing made his stomach drop. He watched two small balls of fur wander through the torn screen door.

The situation had just gone from serious to dangerous.

"B-bear." Hannah shook beside him.

"Don't scream." He pulled her into his arms. The two cubs sniffed the air and looked toward them. "Back slowly toward the kitchen and get in the utility closet." Logan waited until she was inside, then said, "Okay, little guys, take this and join Mama outside." He took the plate of bacon off the table and tossed it toward the cubs and followed Hannah into the closet.

Darkness enveloped them.

He held Hannah in his arms; he could feel her heart beating rapidly. Or was that his?

"What are we going to do?" she whispered against his chest.

He hated the fear in her voice. "We could make out," he teased. "It's been years since I've been in a closet with a girl."

She punched him in the stomach, but he didn't mind. He'd rather have her angry than scared.

"I'm serious, Logan."

He didn't say that he was too. "Sorry, I was trying to distract you. Don't worry. They'll leave soon." The crash of pans made him a liar.

Hannah buried her face in his chest. "I can't help thinking they're going to break down the door any moment."

"Don't worry, we're safe," he stroked her hair in an attempt to comfort her. "Try to think about something else."

Logan searched his brain for a solution. Holding Hannah in his arms wasn't the worst way to spend a morning, but he didn't like that she jumped at every sound coming from outside the closet. He didn't have his bear spray; it was in his fishing vest on the porch.

So for now, they were trapped.

"Why..." Hannah's soft voice vibrated on his chest. "Why didn't you kiss me last night?"

Logan stopped stroking her hair. He'd suggested she think about something else and she picked a subject that would definitely distract them. He looked down, but could only make out her outline. "I..." *was afraid I wouldn't want to stop.* He couldn't say that. "Did you want me to kiss you?"

"Well..." She buried her face in his chest and her words came out muffled. "Only if you wanted to?"

Logan felt his ears heat, and his whole body followed. He reached down and found the contours of her face. He lifted her chin. "I wanted to do more than kiss you." He couldn't make out her features but it didn't matter; he already knew them. "But so much time has passed... I wasn't sure if I was alone in—"

"You weren't." Her hand touched his cheek. "You're not alone."

It was all the invitation he needed. Logan reached down and found her lips with his and sealed them together. It had been two year but her touch still sent a spark through him. He lifted her up and pressed her against the door. This was nothing like their previous kiss so many years ago; this wasn't a gentle request. This kiss was a declaration. A beginning.

* * *

"Logan? Miss Summers?" Jake called out. "Is anyone in here?"

Logan raised his head from the back wall of the closet. It took him a second to get his bearings after falling asleep. Jake wasn't supposed to stop by until Sunday. How long had they been trapped? When had the bears left? He hadn't heard—

"I saw a family of black bears running from the cabin," Jake explained.

So they hadn't been trapped long—a few hours maybe. But the warm curvy body in Logan's lap made him think it hadn't been long enough. He touched Hannah's shoulder to wake her. "The bears are gone." He couldn't help that he sounded disappointed.

Hannah slid from his arms and knelt next to him. "I can't believe we made out while bears ransacked your cabin." She started to giggle. "I guess your suggestion wasn't as bad as it seemed."

"Are you guys okay?" Jake said, approaching.

"Yeah, we'll be right out." Logan answered. He looked at the woman who two years ago had piqued his interest and in less than twenty-four hours had stolen his heart. "Marry me."

"No way." She continued to giggle. "How about dinner back in the city?"

"Dinner at a hotel on the way back?"

Hannah shook her head. "Are we going to argue the entire time we're dating?"

"No." Logan pressed his forehead against hers. "We're going to argue the rest of our lives."

She put her hand on his cheek. "Deal."

First Date Fiasco

Sarah Alva

When Eleanor Lavish walked into his sister's engagement party, Freddy Kappal couldn't decide if he should hide in the bushes or walk right up and tell her what's what. He hadn't seen Ellie in months. Nine months and two days, actually. Not that he had been keeping track. He'd heard a few months ago that she had moved to Salt Lake, but had given up hope he'd ever run into her.

Freddy busied himself getting a lemonade. When the shock of seeing her again disappeared, he decided to play it cool. No need to let her know he'd thought of her every day since they'd met at his aunt's Christmas party last year. And there was definitely no need for her to know how much her rejection had stung. Best to act indifferent.

Ellie was talking with Freddy's cousin Charlotte and sister, Lucy. Freddy took a sip of his lemonade then set it down before heading toward the women.

"And Freddy will still be there after I get married," Lucy said.

"Did someone say my name?" he asked, draping his arms over Lucy and Charlotte's shoulders. He didn't even glance in Ellie's direction. He was killing the cool and casual vibe.

"I'm trying to convince Charlotte to be your neighbor," Ellie said.

He flicked his eyes in her direction and nearly lost his breath. Eleanor Lavish was still the most beautiful woman he'd ever seen. The sunlight behind her pulled out red tones in her dark hair and shadowed her face in intense angles. Her lush red lips hinted at a smirk.

"Eleanor," Freddy said. His voice sounded cold. Angry. Not the cool indifference he'd been aiming for. He dropped his arms from his sister and cousin. "It's been a few months."

The air vibrated between them. Ellie's gaze grew hard. Penetrative. Then she smiled. A cruel, red smile. Freddy heard Lucy excuse herself, and Charlotte drifted after her, leaving him and Ellie alone in a staring contest.

"You never answered my calls or texts," he said.

"I think you know why," she replied. She brushed a lock of hair away from her face.

There were three reasons he suspected she had never called him back. The first, he'd scared her off. He'd been in a really dark place when they met at the Christmas party. And he might have overshared some super personal things with her. But he thought they'd made a real connection because she was the one who had kissed him, even after all the TMIing.

Second, she'd forgotten who he was. It was not totally unreasonable to assume she'd forgotten some rando she met at a party, even if they had made out.

Third, she really was as cold and emotionally unavailable as she claimed to be. She didn't call him back because she had a mean streak and wanted to hurt him. Or she was trying to protect herself.

"I actually don't know why you never called," Freddy said. He crossed his arms over his chest. The tension between them was doing some weird stuff to his body. His heart felt like it was trying to break out of his chest and his pits had become total swamps. "Why don't you tell me?"

She tipped her head to the side and looked at him like she was studying a piece of art. A silver earring swung back and forth between her loose hair and her neck. "You look good, Freddy," she said. Her compliment made his neck warm. But he couldn't let her misdirect him.

"How have you been?" she asked, then smiled innocently. "Isn't that what people usually say when they haven't seen each other in a while?"

Freddy ground his teeth together. "Yes, that's what people usually say. But we're not usual people, are we?"

Her lip tugged up in one corner. "Why don't you get me a drink and we can catch up?"

Freddy had a feeling if he turned his back to her, she'd disappear. So he walked backward to the refreshment table, keeping his eyes locked on her. He slammed into something. A table. The church ladies seated at the table gasped. Turning to the women, he flashed his most charming smile. "Apologies, matrons." He whipped his head back in Ellie's direction, fully expecting her to be gone. Instead, he caught her mid-laugh.

Once she realized he was watching, she covered her mouth with a hand, and her face became a mask of boredom. She shooed him with her hand to continue. He turned and made it to the refreshment table in two big steps, then promptly turned back to her. *Of course, Ellie was gone.* He sighed. *Figures.*

Freddy picked up a pink macaron and shoved it whole in his mouth.

"You're taking too long."

Freddy jumped and gasped, bits of macaron shooting down his throat. Ellie had appeared out of nowhere. Freddy coughed and pounded on his chest. "Water," he rasped. *Oh good.* If he could speak, that meant his airway wasn't completely cut off.

Ellie ladled a cup full of lemonade and passed it over to him. She looked totally unconcerned that he was having a near-death experience. Freddy glugged the drink down, coughed and gagged a few more times, then cleared his throat. "Thanks," he mumbled when he could breathe again. Freddy was usually a smooth operator when it came to women. Ellie turned him into a bit of an idiot.

Ellie handed him a napkin. "Congratulations, Freddy. It looks like you'll live to see another day."

He laughed dryly. "Would you still like something to drink?"

"Hmm. These macarons sure look good." She picked a pink one and bit into it, batting her eyelashes as she chewed. She was teasing him. That was good, right? Or was this a prelude to something mean?

He got her a cup of lemonade and motioned with his head toward an empty table. Ellie grabbed a few more cookies and followed him. Freddy set the drinks down and pulled out her chair. Ellie wore a red dress that was cut pretty high above her knees. As she sat in her chair, she made a show of crossing her legs. She smirked when she caught him watching. Freddy's neck warmed again. Get it together, man.

He took the chair beside her and fingered his cup of lemonade. "I've thought a lot about you," he said. Then instantly wanted to die. That was the exact thing he was not supposed to say.

"I'm sure you have." She toyed with the jeweled pendant on her necklace, drawing his gaze down. "And what exactly have you been thinking?"

Freddy swallowed and pulled away from her. He didn't want to get to know this version of Ellie. The vixen. The seductress. The version he'd heard rumors about. He wanted to know better the Ellie he'd met at Christmas, the one who could be vulnerable and understanding. The one who kissed him even after he told her the worst thing about himself.

"That I want to get to know you better," he said.

She shook her head. "Come on, Freddy. You remember the Christmas party. I'm a disaster."

"Let me decide if you're too much of a disaster for me."

She bit her bottom lip and Freddy remembered vividly how soft her mouth had felt against his. She turned her head away.

Freddy moved closer to her. "Ellie, look at me." He placed a finger on her chin and coaxed her face forward. Fear made her eyes wide. She pulled back and blinked. Her face became a mask. "Let me get to know you."

"You're wasting your time." Her voice held a cold edge.

"One date," he said. "And if it's totally horrible and we really don't make a connection, I'll leave you alone."

She folded her arms over her chest.

"At least return my call this time," he said.

Her arms dropped with a sigh. "Fine."

Freddy grinned. Small victories.

She rolled her eyes and stood. Freddy watched her walk across the yard for a beat longer than was polite.

* * *

He called forty-eight hours later, and now Ellie sat in Freddy's old Honda at 6:17 pm on a Friday night.

They were driving to the west side of the valley. Ellie purposely hadn't asked any questions about where they were going and what they were doing. She didn't want to appear too interested or invested. She made polite, first date conversation. Nothing close to the deep, probing discussions they'd fallen into last Christmas. Ellie was determined to squash Freddy's interest in her. She was a capital "M" mess with ridiculous amounts of emotional baggage. A nice guy like Freddy didn't need to take her on. She shouldn't have even agreed to this date in the first place, but when she was with Freddy, the pressure in her chest lessened. She felt tugs of hope and happiness. And for someone who had spent so much of the last decade feeling dark and heavy, she couldn't resist a little light.

"I read one of your books," he said after a too-long silence.

"Yeah?" She'd forgotten she'd told him her pen name. Starlit Knight. "Which one?"

"Um, *Her Bad Boy Billionaire Mistake*."

The titles always made her cringe, but it was all about marketing.

"And what did you think?" she asked. For some reason, she wanted him to have liked it. Yeah, on the surface her books were steamy romance novels, but she tried to be a little more thematically ambitious than was expected for the genre.

"It was..." He glanced at her. Did she look too eager? "I had to skip a lot of it, because I worried all the sexiness would be triggering. But I enjoyed it."

It jarred her how causally he'd brought up his porn addiction. It was the admission of his struggle that'd sent their very first conversation to the deep end. He'd shared his secret shame, so she'd shared one of hers.

Freddy pulled into a small shopping center with a Mexican grocery store and a few restaurants. He parked the car in front of an empty store front. "Shoot. It looks like the restaurant closed down."

He drummed his fingers on the steering wheel a few times, looking at the other restaurants. Flashing her a smile, he got out of the car to open her door. "We'll just pick one of these other places to eat." Ellie slung her purse over her shoulder. She looked over the marquees of the other restaurants.

"How about Bucket 'o Crawfish?" Freddy suggested. Oh great. Was he trying to make this date memorable by making it as weird as possible?

"I'm actually allergic to shellfish," Ellie said. Which was the truth, thank goodness. Through the window she could see people eating off the tables with their hands.

"Okay," Freddy said, a determined smile on his face. "Thai or pho?" he asked, gesturing to the two other restaurants.

Ellie didn't like either, but if she had to choose... "Pho, I guess."

"Don't sound too excited," Freddy playfully bumped her shoulder.

* * *

Freddy watched Ellie stir her pho with the big white plastic spoon. He'd devoured his soup between their stifled bits of conversation. He hadn't eaten since breakfast and had been starving. But now that his bowl was empty, he realized Ellie must not have taken more than a few sips. He should have read her lack of enthusiasm for what it was and taken her to eat somewhere else. This date was not going like he imagined.

"What's your favorite fast food restaurant?" Freddy asked.

Ellie looked up from her large bowl of pho. "Are you going to make fun of my answer?"

He grinned. "Me? I never make fun of anyone."

She rolled her eyes.

"Look," he said. "I can tell you don't like your food. Let me at least get you your favorite low-quality hamburger."

"Or taco?" she asked, lifting an eyebrow.

"Or taco." Freddy signaled the server. The server set the check on the table and Freddy opened his wallet. The slot where his debit card usually sat was empty. Shoot. He'd ordered something online last night and must not have put it back. And he only had twenty dollars cash.

"So, funny story." He expected Ellie to wear the disdainful bored look she'd given him plenty of times. Instead, her mouth was down-turned in sympathy.

"How about I get dinner, and you pay for my Taco Bell?" she said. Before he could protest, she put her credit card on the table with the check.

Soon, they were walking back to his car. Freddy's heart beat erratically. Ellie had been nice to him even though he'd done the stupidest thing. And he couldn't help but hope that meant she did like him after all.

* * *

Ellie did not moan with pleasure as she bit into her low-quality taco. Nor did she wax poetic about the amazingness that was the Chalupa. Freddy drove them back to the east side of the valley as she ate. She didn't ask if the date was over, and also didn't acknowledge the tug of disappointment if it was. If Freddy was really trying to win her over, surely the date wouldn't end after a Taco Bell run.

Her disappointment solidified when they pulled into his apartment complex. They'd met at his place for the date because she didn't want her roommates making a big deal about her going out.

Freddy parked the car then angled himself to look at her. Suddenly he was leaning toward her and Ellie instinctively moved back, hitting the car window. Was he serious?

Freddy grinned and ran his finger through the ends of her hair. Between his fingers he held up a piece of lettuce. "You're a pretty sloppy eater for someone so poised."

Oh. He wasn't going to kiss her. She tucked her hair behind her ear and looked down. Her lap was covered in lettuce and cheese. *Great.*

Freddy popped his car door open. "You ready for Part II?"

"Part II?" She dusted the cheese and lettuce into the Taco Bell bag.

"You thought the night was over?"

She willed herself not to smile. With a shrug, she opened her door before Freddy got the chance to get it for her. He came around to her side.

"You should probably check your hair for cheese," he said.

Her hand flew into her hair and she bent down to look at herself in the side mirror. Freddy laughed and she cut him a look.

"Let's stroll," he said.

Freddy offered her arm and she looped her wrist through. "Stroll?"

He led them from the parking lot up toward the busy street by his apartment. "Lots of questions," he said. "But I'm surprised you're not sharing your opinion."

"Maybe I'm just being polite and accommodating."

"Good," he said, "because we're going to a couples massage next."

Ellie's stomach dipped in disappointment. How silly of her to think Freddy was different from all the other guys who pursued her. Perhaps it was best to give him what he wanted. Maybe if he slept with her, he'd get it out of his system and leave her alone. "I usually don't take off my clothes until the end of the date." She moved closer to him and made sure her breast brushed against his arm. "But okay."

Freddy stopped walking and turned to her. His gray eyes were as sharp as their steely color. "That's not what I want from you," he said, voice low.

His sudden intensity had her heart racing. She swallowed, hoping he didn't notice how he affected her. She didn't dare ask the question on the tip of her tongue: *What do you want from me?* Instead, she put on her best Cheshire smile. "Then why are we getting a couples massage?"

"We aren't," he said. "I forgot the silly things I say don't scandalize you."

Ellie got his subtext. He usually dated nice girls he could tease by saying outrageous things. Ellie had taken him at his word because that's the kind of thing the guys she usually dated would have offered.

"Freddy, what are we doing?" She'd meant it to be a general question, but her voice had a vulnerable catch. She was clearly asking something different.

He smiled. Tender. His eyes warm. She wanted to hate how he made hope flicker in her chest. "We're going on a stroll," he said.

* * *

Freddy offered his arm again, but she didn't take it. He tried not to read too much into it. Ellie was a mystery and unpredictable, and she never said what she really meant and never did what she was expected to. It was part of her allure and he was feeling more and more foolish by the moment for thinking he'd be the one she'd be real with. Again.

They walked a few blocks in awkward silence. They stopped at a crosswalk and Freddy pushed the button. "Have you been to Allen Park?" he asked.

"Nope," she replied. The crosswalk beeped, and Ellie walked ahead. Perhaps a couples massage would have been a better idea. At least they'd have been in the same room and she wouldn't have been able to get away from him.

Freddy took two big steps and caught up to her. Once they were safely across the street, he grabbed her by the elbow to stop her. She spun around, her eyes cool. "If you're unhappy with me, we can end our stroll."

She sighed. "No, it's fine. I'm being rude. Tell me about Allen Park."

Freddy gestured to a gated street a few paces away. "This is Allen Park."

He offered his arm again and she took it this time. They stepped through the gate and started up the street.

"It's not really a park," she said as they walked by a dilapidated house.

"This eccentric doctor and his family owned this land for a long time. He rented the houses on the property. He was also an artist." Freddy gestured to a peacock mosaic pressed into concrete. "And he liked poetry and left quotes all over." Ellie left his side to take a closer look at the mosaic. "Since you're a writer, I thought you'd like the poetry." Freddy gave a little shrug, certain he'd made the wrong move with her.

She looked at him over her shoulder. "Let's keep walking," she said.

They started up the street, toward the main house. The air was filled with the sound of birds and the gurgle of a creek. When he reached for Ellie's hand, she didn't pull away; instead, she laced her fingers through his.

* * *

Up ahead, a peacock strutted down the street. "Is that a..." Ellie stopped and squeezed Freddy's hand. A familiar terror clenched her legs.

"Yeah. The doctor bred them or something."

"Oh."

Ellie stepped to the side as the peacock came closer. The bird stopped and bobbed his head up and down. A cold chill slinked down her spine as his small beady eyes looked her over. He took a few steps back, then puffed out his chest and fanned out his tail feathers.

"He likes you," Freddy said with a laugh.

"Let's keep walking," she mumbled and made a wide berth around the bird.

The peacock let out a horrible squawk and strutted after them. "Oh my… he's following us," Ellie said, trying to tap down her hysteria.

"No, he's following you." Freddy laughed again.

Ellie worried the bird would fly after her if she tried to run, but continuing to walk felt just as dangerous.

The bird took quick steps toward them and Ellie darted behind Freddy's back to hide. She peeked over his shoulder to see the peacock still advancing. She ducked down and grabbed a handful of his shirt. "Freddy, do something!" Her voice was shrill and Freddy laughed. AGAIN. Ellie pressed her face into his back. "It's almost like you're enjoying this!"

"Maybe a little," he said, glancing at her over his shoulder.

She swatted his back. A back and shoulders that were extremely muscular. *Huh.*

"I'm terrified of birds," Ellie said, stealing another look over his shoulder.

"I gathered that," Freddy replied.

The peacock spun in a slow circle so Ellie could see all of his feathers. "Okay. When his back is to us," Freddy said in a whisper, "We'll make a run for it."

Ellie nodded, her heart pounding in her throat. She watched the bird, Freddy her only protection. When the peacock's slow dance revealed his behind, Ellie ran for the exit, a loud shriek ripping from her throat. This was in the top ten most embarrassing moments of her life and one of the worst dates she'd ever been on.

* * *

Freddy grabbed Ellie's hand as they fled the park. A quick glance over his shoulder revealed the peacock was not in pursuit, which was good. Because Freddy did not want to be upstaged by a bird. This date was going terribly and an amorous bird trying to mate with his date was not the thing he needed right now.

They ran for a good two blocks before Freddy slowed down. Her hand tugged out of his, but she stopped a few paces ahead. She took in deep breaths with her hands on her knees.

"You okay?" he asked.

She shook her head and stood up straight. "I'm fine."

Her cheeks had turned a cute shade of pink and her hair had gone a little wild.

"Should we try for Part III, or are you ready to call it quits?" Freddy asked, hoping his cheeky smile covered how desperate he was. Part III was his last chance to save this horrible night.

Ellie fanned her face. "Yeah. Might as well see this through."

What a cheery vote of confidence.

They walked the few blocks back to his apartment. He didn't bother explaining he was not inviting her in to make out. He figured she either knew him or didn't.

"My sister is an ice cream scientist," he said as he opened the door. "But I think you know that."

"Yes," Ellie said. Freddy tossed his keys on the bar in the kitchen.

"She usually has samples of her latest concoctions in the freezer."

Freddy opened the freezer door and began pulling out white cartons of ice cream. Ellie picked one up and read the words written in Sharpie, "Lavender Love."

"Do you want a cone or a bowl?"

"A cone," Ellie said, picking up another carton. "Will Lucy mind if we eat her ice cream?"

"She'll thank us," Freddy said, searching the cabinets for the cones. "If I don't eat it, then she does. And then I get in trouble for not doing my part."

Ellie didn't even offer him a small chuckle. Instead, she sorted through the ice cream cartons with unnatural attention. She'd sent him mixed signals all night. If she started to have fun, she'd stop herself. But when he offered her an out, she didn't take it. Now, he felt her pulling away. He wondered if she even knew what she wanted.

He found the ice cream cones, then grabbed a scooper. "Anything look good?"

Ellie held up a carton: Peanut Butter Brownie Batter. She smiled weakly. Like she wanted to try, but it was too hard. Or too scary.

He wasn't going to be able to save this date. Ellie wasn't going to let him in, either.

* * *

Freddy handed over her ice cream cone, then scooped himself one of the same flavor. Ellie looked at her glistening chocolate ice cream. A tightness was returning to her chest. A tightness that was always there. Except it hadn't been there the last two hours.

Freddy threw the ice cream back in the freezer. "Let's eat at the gazebo," he said.

They left his apartment and went to the courtyard. The gazebo was a beautiful white with ornate scrolling on the posts and eves. They sat on a wicker bench. Ellie shifted so their elbows wouldn't bump as they ate (Freddy was a lefty), but their elbows bummed anyway. The top scoop on her ice cream cone went tumbling and landed on Freddy's shoe.

Freddy let out a defeated sigh. "I should have seen that coming," he said.

Ellie felt a laugh knocking around in her chest. She pressed her lips together to keep it in. Freddy cut her a look and she tried to sober up but she cracked. First, small, contained giggles. But soon it was like someone had shook a soda and she couldn't stop. Freddy started laughing too. She never laughed like this. Ever. Tears streamed down Ellie's face. And that tightness in her chest vanished again.

Ellie wiped her eyes and looked over at Freddy. Seeing him smiling like that made her stomach flip. She took a few deep breaths and got herself under control.

"So," Freddy said. "Was this a *great date*? Or *the greatest date ever*?" He gave her a self-deprecating grin.

"Oh, definitely *the greatest date ever*. On a *great date*, I was courted by a roadrunner, so a peacock is a total step up."

"Don't forget the low-quality tacos," Freddy added.

"Absolutely. Mexican-adjacent food is my favorite."

They shared a smile and the warning bells went off inside her. She wasn't supposed to be flirting with him. She was supposed to be cold and indifferent so he wouldn't pursue her anymore. She had every reason and opportunity to. This was, on paper, a very bad date. But... darn it, she liked spending time with him. She liked that he didn't make her feel broken. She liked that he could make her laugh. That she had to work really hard to be mean to him. He brought out her better self. Ellie felt like the person she always wished she could be when she was with him.

"I'm gonna change my shoes. I'll be right back," he said.

Ellie nodded and watched him walk away, longing tugging in her stomach.

By the time he returned, she'd finished what was left of her ice cream cone. "Can I walk you to your car?" he asked.

Ellie nodded, a little disappointed that their time together was ending.

His hand found hers as they walked across the parking lot. They stopped in front of her car. "So, how does the *greatest date ever* end?" He lifted an eyebrow and his fingers played against hers. The heat in his gray eyes ticked her pulse up. Ellie knew how she would typically end a date, *greatest ever*, or not. But Freddy was different, and she was already at her car.

She tipped her head. "*Great dates* end with a hand shake."

Freddy took a small step toward her. "And *greatest dates ever*?" His hand came up and pushed aside a lock of her hair. A delicious shiver raced down her spine. Her lips warmed as his eyes drifted down to her mouth.

"To get a kiss, Freddy," she hooked a finger between the buttons of his shirt. "This would need to be *the greatest date* of all time."

The rumble of his laugh did strange things to her.

"Then a hug for *the greatest date ever*?" he asked.

She tugged his shirt forward and stepped into his arm. It took her a nanosecond to realize she should have opted for the kiss. Being wrapped in his embrace, his breath on her cheek, her arms secured around his neck, felt much more intimate than a kiss. She could feel the rise and fall of his chest against hers. She could smell the scent of his skin beneath his cologne. He started to pull away but Ellie held him tighter. "Not yet," she whispered.

Freddy felt like the home she always wanted, filled with the love she never had. And she didn't want to let go.

Edgar's Ghost Girlfriend

Liz Christensen

Edgar wasn't afraid of ghosts. He believed in them too much. The one that swayed the front porch swing at twilight he believed in most of all. He was in love with her.

He had been unhappily single when he moved into the bungalow at the end of Coleman Field. It was spacious for such a cheap rental, probably because it was plonked down in the middle of nowhere rural Sucksville. Edgar had signed the lease without much attention to the other details. Within budget? Check. Far from Clicksy Court Condos but still within a thirty-minute commute to the warehouse? Check. Not likely to run into any of Alicia's friends or family? Double-check that. This place squatted solidly between cows and alfalfa for neighbors. Definitely not Alicia's style. In his affinity for horror films, Edgar realized no one lived close enough to hear him scream.

The haunting began his very first night in the house, though Edgar didn't realize it. He assumed the front porch swing was squeaking because of the wind. The next night was the same. About a week later, Edgar was retrieving an Amazon package from the end of the driveway, muttering about how it shouldn't be that hard to drop the box off at the porch, when he finally noticed it. The front porch swing was squeaking and swaying. It was more annoying than anything, a very grating sound. But as Edgar set the package on the porch to open the door, the swing came to an abrupt stop. *That was weird.* Edgar turned the knob, opened the front door, picked up his package, and went inside. As soon as the door was shut, Edgar heard the rhythmic irritant again. He set the package in the hall and yanked open the front door. The swing froze. Edgar stared back at it with wide eyes. Edgar pursed his lips and furrowed his eyebrows. He leaned against the door frame, letting the stuffy air from inside mingle with the country air outside.

Edgar folded his arms.

"Go on then, don't mind me," he joked.

He didn't laugh as the bench seat slid forward and down into a more natural stopped position.

Edgar's breath escaped from his nostrils.

He blinked. He couldn't possibly have seen what he thought he saw, right?

A hesitant swing forward and back. It built momentum with each successive raise and persuaded Edgar that he did see what he thought he saw.

"Oh, well, good. Glad to see it's still working like it should," he babbled, backing into the house and closing the door with one hand on the knob, the other pressing firmly on the door jam. A deep breath in and out through the mouth, and Edgar locked the deadbolt.

Every night after sunset, the front porch swing would rock. Edgar experimented with watching from the window, coming around the side of the house, sitting on the sorry excuse for a front lawn, and eventually sitting on the front steps. Conversation, tentative at first and decidedly one-sided, happened like low-pressure water from a garden hose. Edgar would gurgle out ridiculous attempts at small talk in fits and starts. The only response in those early days was the occasional pause of the swing. Edgar would flush, then go overthink alone in the house, wondering what he had said wrong.

He would never have considered crushing on the ghost if she hadn't started it. Edgar was on his way to the front porch steps from the detached garage. He was late getting home from work and was in a bad mood. He hated when things at the warehouse got so backlogged that he had to drive home in the dark. Coleman Field didn't receive the maintenance other roads in the county received and it was a long and narrow lane. Even though he had the potholes pretty well memorized, the car always seemed to find something unexpected to complain about in the home stretch of his commute. Edgar was distracted thinking about when the car would finally give up on him, just like Alicia.

Deep in thought, he turned the corner to the front porch sharply.

The swing rattled into action.

Edgar paused, door key in hand, mouth agape.

The swing squeaked with vigor in an insistent rhythm.

Edgar was certain the swing hadn't started until it had seen him. Had he taken it by surprise? It was well after dark, but it hadn't been swinging until he arrived. Had it been waiting for him?

Edgar flushed. "Sorry I'm late. Work was stupid," he mumbled.

The swing eased into a consistent rhythm with less persistence.

Edgar sat on the front steps, thinking about the swing, but keeping his eyes on the door key in his hand.

"I don't even like my job really. I just don't want to look for another right now, you know?"

The swing creaked slightly. Edgar looked up. The bench seemed tilted a little. On one side the chains were taut as could be, but the other side looked a little slack. Edgar wasn't alarmed. *There is weight to it after all*, he thought. He figured as much. Something about fulcrum physics nonsense he hadn't thought about since high school. He wasn't really surprised that whatever weight made the swing sway could scoot to one side. It was clearly a two-seater bench. Edgar told himself it wasn't weird, and took a cautious seat on the slack side of the bench. The swing balanced, and Edgar relaxed.

He talked on and on that night. Somehow it was easy. Alicia would always interrupt, or switch the conversation to herself. Edgar hated the sound of his own voice. He never sang in the shower or the car. Somehow, none of that mattered. The swing rocked him and never interrupted once. He told the air about his job, his breakup, his car troubles, the ongoing fight with the hot water handle in the bathroom inside, and his incredulity that pizza delivery would charge him an extra ten dollars to come to this location. He talked so long, he missed dinner and didn't mind.

When he had said all he needed to say, he realized he wanted to ask a question. He had no idea how to phrase it.

"Thank you," he began, "for listening. For waiting up for me."

Edgar looked at the air next to him over the bench. The swing had become very still. Edgar flushed. *What idiot talks to the air?* He stood. The chains jerked taut on one end and rattled slackened on the other with the change of weight. A warm breeze brushed his arm, and Edgar felt something soft against his leg as the bench slid from a sloped angle to something more parallel with the porch.

He didn't flinch. He just felt. Eyes open, deep, quiet breathing through the nose, all his senses reached out. He didn't notice the smell of the cows. He didn't notice the cooling temperature of autumn after dark. He didn't notice the lone mosquito wafting around the porch pillar. What he did notice was regard. It regarded him. He flushed. It felt like the warm breeze curled around his arm.

"Goodnight," he stammered and went for the door.

The swing began a lazy rock as he unlocked the house and went inside.

It wasn't until after he closed the front door that Edgar realized the squeaking no longer bothered him.

Edgar began to care about the view of his yard and home from the porch. When he wasn't working, he swept, pulled weeds, and painted trim. The evening and night hours were spent on the porch swing. He began swinging later and sleeping less, until he was put on report for a minor incident at work with the forklift due to his exhaustion. That's when he told his crush they needed to implement a date night curfew. He may not love his job, but he did need it.

On the porch swing, Edgar never ran out of conversation, and he realized he was funny, creative, and articulate. He told his swingmate about his idea for a video game and developed it over the next few weeks. He knew he had it when in the middle of wrapping up some loose ends about his idea, the bench bucked and Edgar gripped the chains to steady himself. It felt as if someone was bouncing up and down in excitement next to him.

"So you think I should do it? Like really pitch Haunted Warehouse to a developer or something?"

The swing chains rattled as the bench rallied in support again.

"Oh, you are the best!" Edgar effused.

The swing stopped. Edgar felt the weight balance of the swing shift in his direction.

A cool softness pressed against his cheek. He knew he had been kissed.

Over the years, the alfalfa and cow pasture around Coleman Field developed. Urban sprawl incorporated Edgar's bungalow rental into the county. When the homeowner decided to sell to a big box housing developer, Edgar outbid the national business. He'd made a fortune on his debut video game, and the fortune grew with each successive release in the series. The bungalow sat, outdated and untouched as stucco behemoths rose up all around it. Edgar didn't mind. There was now better maintenance of the asphalt.

The neighborhood kids grew very fond of the man at the end of the road. He spent every night on his porch swing talking to himself, which meant he was obviously crazy. But he was kind to them. He was always in his front yard in the late afternoons and evenings, watering the garden, painting the trim, preparing like the Queen of England would be coming to make a visit. He would wave to the kids on scooters or playing kick the can. He never scolded when they hid behind his hedges in his front yard during hide-and-seek—unless they played after sunset. He knew their names, gave out the best candy on Halloween, and told incredible stories.

The adult neighbors admired him too. Even though his house was out of fashion, Edgar was careful to keep it fixed up. Especially everything that could be seen from the curb. He was an ideal neighbor, unassuming and orderly. When word broke among the teenagers that he was the creator of the Haunted Warehouse, the adults were more impressed. Edgar was rich, but even a passing glance at his home and lifestyle showed he was humble. Too bad he was so alone. No family ever came to visit. Edgar never let anyone set him up on a date. He was growing old and alone at the end of Coleman Field. And yet he was the most content person the neighborhood had ever known. And why shouldn't he be? Amazon packages were now delivered to the steps, and pizza delivery came with no additional charges. And best of all, every night, the porch swing rocked.

Where Main Street Meets Tomorrow

Bryan Young

Working graveyard shifts had always been Carol's favorite. They were quiet, and if they were dead enough, she could get her history homework done. The pancake restaurant was across from the famous storybook park with its magical rides and dressed up actors, often portraying popular characters from famous novels and movies.

Late at night, it was only the most hungry and exhausted of tourists that filtered in. Invariably, one of the adults would be carrying a zonked-out child in mouse ears in their arms, and Carol would seat them in the largest booth. That way, the poor kids could sleep in peace. Occasionally, though, cast members, weary from long days of cultivating happiness, would filter inside in twos and threes complaining about the pay and swapping stories about interactions they had, both the good and the bad.

On that particular night, the diner was quiet. There were three people inside. Carol, nose buried in a textbook, the manager napping in the office, and Lewis, the cook in the kitchen, playing on his phone the entire time.

The door chimed, and Carol looked up from her notes to see a woman. Petite. Blonde hair. Blue eyes. A soft face that faked a smile when their eyes met.

Her eyes were red and puffy, and the mascara smeared down her face in inky drips. Definitely not in a way that could have been mistaken for fashionable. No, something had happened to her, but Carol didn't want to ask what. Instead, she stood and greeted her.

"Just take a seat here," Carol said, directing her to the most out-of-the-way booth in the diner, just to give her some semblance of privacy. "Do you need anything? I'll bring a water, but do you need anything stronger? Coffee? Tea?"

"Tea, please," she squeaked, her voice ready to crack with emotion.

She settled into the booth while Carol bustled to the drink station, preparing the little box of teabags to bring out before filling the kettle with hot water.

The stranger sat there, drying her eyes, and Carol's heart couldn't help but break for the young woman. No one should ever have to be that sad. Especially by themselves and in the middle of the night.

It was no way to while away the time.

Carol placed the tea kettle gently in front of the poor girl.

"You have a chance to look at the menu?" Carol knew she hadn't, but her script was so ingrained that it was difficult to fight against. Especially in the middle of the night. And her paper was due the next day, and she had to get it finished. "We've got some specials tonight…"

The girl nodded and looked up into Carol's eyes. Carol felt a spark, a connection, something she hadn't felt in a long time. And it came directly from this girl with the blue eyes, tinged crimson with tears.

She shoved away the attraction. Dating was too hard between work and school and surviving. She was busting her ass, and what right did this girl have to come in and threaten to upend that?

Carol took a breath, waiting for the girl to respond. She felt the inexplicable urge to offer more than the polite script and standard emotional labor. Exhaustion came in managing the emotional space of a customer that she had to save for homework, but there was something about this girl.

"I don't know," the woman said. "Just… pancakes, I guess? Blueberry."

"Short stack or tall stack?"

She shrugged. "Tall?"

"You got it."

Carol went to the computer at the drink station and tapped in Lewis' marching orders, but she couldn't stop stealing glances at her guest. The woman worked to dry her eyes and clean the running makeup from her face with one of the rough napkins from the table.

Carol dug inside her backpack and pulled out a package of makeup removers and Kleenex. She walked it over and slid them onto the table. She didn't want to make a big deal about it, but she knew that the act of being nice might actually make her cry harder. The poor thing was already having a rough enough time. She didn't need the added, awkward pressure of having to make small talk with a server. Carol already knew how much that small talk exhausted her from the other side of that equation. Especially since dudes never had a clue. And they could never take the hint that Carol wasn't interested.

Carol was already halfway across the restaurant when she heard the woman say "Thank you" in a small, quiet voice. A voice laced with a need to talk. It was unmistakable. That sad warble that said, *Pay attention to me, please. It may not look like it, but that's what I need.*

So Carol turned back to the only table with a guest to see what she could do.

"You okay?" Carol asked.

She expected to hear one of the standard, obligatory but non-committal responses. "I'm fine." Or "I'm okay." Or "All right." Or one of a hundred empty platitudes humans use to deflect when they don't want to talk about what's bothering them.

Least of all with a stranger.

"No," was all the girl said. Simple and soft.

Carol wasn't sure if she should push further or not. Instead, she opted for her old chestnut of a work-related question. "You need anything?"

If the girl wanted to open up, the invitation was there, or she could simply ask Carol to go away on a fetch quest.

"I need to listen to myself more," she said.

And that gave Carol her cue. Her homework wasn't going to finish itself, but if she could help just by listening in the dead of night, then that's what Carol would do. The Battle of Hastings hadn't changed in a thousand years, what was a few more minutes? "What do you mean?"

"I give myself good advice, and I just need to follow it."

"Who hurt you?" Carol said. She practically blurted it before she knew she had, but it felt right when it came out.

"It was nothing. It's done anyway. She left."

"Tonight?"

The young woman nodded. "She sent a message. She didn't even call."

"I'm sorry."

"Me too." She wiped her eyes again as more tears threatened to drown her.

Carol didn't know what else to say but was saved by Lewis' dinging bell. "Order up!"

He slid the tall stack of blueberry pancakes through the window and disappeared into the kitchen.

Carol fetched the pancakes and carrier of warm syrups as the girl fixed her tea, tearing open a packet of English breakfast and pouring steaming water over it inside her brown, porcelain cup.

"Here you go," Carol said, dropping the pancakes on the table.

Carol figured there were worse things the poor woman could stress eat in the throes of a breakup. Especially one that seemed as sad as the one she looked to be experiencing.

Carol had taken her last breakup just as hard. Breakups seemed to shatter more than hearts, but futures too. Every life's dream cracked like seven years of looking glass.

Carol had done that once and hadn't let it happen again. It was the summer between high school and college and they'd had to keep it a secret. Nicole hadn't been out with her family. And they were both just kids. Nicole's family didn't believe in folks like them. Like their daughter. They'd become invisible.

An upside-down way of thinking.

After a lot of crying, just like Carol's guest, Carol had realized that it made sense. Nicole's family wasn't ready to face the truth of their daughter; they'd rather see in black and white than in a rainbow. And Nicole wasn't ready to give up her family, beneficial as that might be.

The stranger blew on the tea and sipped at it, then set the cup down to dig into her grief-pancakes.

Carol felt a tinge of relief as the tight sadness left the young woman's face as she inhaled her food.

That brought her a smile.

"Just let me know if you need anything else, okay?"

Her mouth stuffed full of cake, the woman nodded. She'd be okay, and it filled Carol with warmth.

When she walked into work that day, Carol would have counted it a victory to just get the shift finished with her paper outlined. But helping this girl felt good, missing half an hour of study time was worth it.

With no one but the girl in the restaurant, Carol figured it would be okay to sit back down and get some of that studying in. At least a few sentences on the paper. But really, if she had to read much more about William the Conqueror, she'd fall asleep then and there, right into a fevered dream and no amount of coffee was going to help.

When the young woman was almost done with her pancakes and tea, Carol forgot about the year 1066 and printed out the check, leaving the tea off the ticket. If there was anything Carol could do, it was to save the girl a few bucks on water and a teabag. She cursed herself for not offering her a slice of pie or something.

"Thank you," the girl said when Carol came by.

"You're very welcome. I hope your night gets better. And there's no rush. Stay as long as you like." Carol barely realized she was offering her warmest smile. She just wanted to pour out as much warmth and empathy as possible, like she was a tea kettle full of comfort, and that was unusual for her. Carol asked herself why, and she noticed the thrill of a crush edging up on her like waves on a beach.

"Thank you," the girl said again.

Shy this time.

Less broken.

Carol's smile broadened. It was all working. She wished she could put a reassuring hand on the girl's shoulder, but there was nothing appropriate or professional about that. Instead, she just cleared the dirty plate and brought it back to the kitchen.

By the time Carol came back out into the dining area, the girl had vanished, leaving only the thought of her smile behind.

It wasn't until Carol bussed the table that she realized there had been something else left there, something more than the trace memory of a lovely, tear-soaked face. There, under the cash left for the bill and a sizable tip, was the receipt. Written on it were some words. And a name and a phone number.

Kathryn.

Carol wondered if she'd have the courage to text Kathryn. Carol had to admit that if it were a guy who had done it, she would have actually been mad. Or at least annoyed. But the bubble lettering that said both, "Thank you," and, "Text me if you want," were just too heartwarming.

It took Carol three days to convince herself to do it.

She had to build up the courage and remind herself that this wasn't some prank. Once had been enough on that score, thank you very much. She also had to convince herself that she had time to fall down that particular rabbit hole. So she made sure she had passed her midterm before texting.

<Kathryn! This is Carol from the diner.>

The response came back quickly. <I'm so glad you texted me! Thanks for being sweet to me that night. I needed it.>

<Not a problem. anyone would have done the same. I hope you're doing better :)>

<I am. Thanks for asking.>

And then Carol froze, unsure of what she should say back. Should she just let it hang there? Or go full-on presumptuous and ask if she wants to hang out? There were too many possibilities.

Carol was grateful her roommates couldn't see her pacing her room in her leopard print robe. She'd told them repeatedly that she wasn't going to get excited about dating until she'd finished her degree, yet here she was, stressing about a pretty girl's texts.

After she'd written and deleted a dozen possible responses, a question arrived on its own.

<you ever go to the park?>

<Not as often as I would like>

<It's magic. Lemme know next time you're coming.>

<I was thinking Saturday, actually> Carol lied.

<That's perfect! Can you be where Main Street meets Tomorrow at 11:15 or so?>

<Anywhere. Any time.>

Carol knew just the spot. It was near the rabbit hole to Alice's Wonderland. She thought she'd be able to scrape up enough scratch to buy a park ticket. She could totally pick up an extra shift.

On Saturday, Carol dressed up in a sundress, pulled her hair into a ponytail, and put on a layer of makeup that she hoped didn't look like she'd put on a layer of makeup.

It was eleven by the time Carol got through the front gate where she left behind Today and delved into Yesterday on her way toward Tomorrow. She took her time wandering up Main Street, hoping she'd arrive at the appointed spot at just the right time.

But she was early.

11:10 by the clock on her phone.

Carol stood by the bathrooms and the painted wooden gate that obscured the park's backstage.

She split her time between watching her phone's clock and scanning the faces in the crowd, searching for Kathryn. She wondered if she'd recognize her without the drowning tears and running makeup. Then she worried that maybe Kathryn wouldn't recognize her.

<I'm here I think> Carol texted, just in case.

But no response came.

"And what's your name, young lady?" a breathlessly high voice asked in a British accent.

Carol looked up to see two men dressed up as Tweedledee and Tweedledum moving around another woman who looked like Alice from Lewis Carroll's *Alice in Wonderland*, standing there with her straight blonde hair in a headband, white tights, and pinafore over a blue dress to match her stunning blue eyes. Carol tilted her head. "Kathryn?"

"Alice is my name," then with a sly smile, Kathryn added, "But Kathryn is a friend of mine. I'm sure the two of you would get along famously."

Kathryn—Alice—smiled a bright, Burbank smile.

"I, uh, I think you're right."

A gate opened and Tweedledee and Tweedledum toddled through, but Alice's smiling face remained. The smile was seductive, landing closer to "come hither" than the Cheshire cat.

"Perhaps," Alice said, "you and I can go to Wonderland together someday. It's such a lovely place. Have you ever been?"

Carol nodded her head and tried keeping her mouth from gaping. "Never."

The White Rabbit passed behind Alice, heading in the same direction as Tweedledee and Tweedledum, checking his clock the entire time.

"I'm ever so late, but Kathryn will contact you soon, young lady, I'm sure, and then to Wonderland you'll go."

Kathryn—Alice—offered a polite curtsy as though Carol were the Queen of Hearts and disappeared backstage, chasing the White Rabbit.

And standing there, in that crossroads where Main Street met Tomorrow, Carol thought about the promise of her own tomorrow. She grinned crookedly, excited to fall down a rabbit hole.

A Fool in Love

Jonathan Reddoch

After I had a sandwich and milk for lunch, I used a quarter to call Dolly. The phone rang a few times before someone answered. I said, "May I speak with Dolly, please?"

I heard a familiar voice say, "This is Dolly." My heart beat faster, my hands were sweating, and my mind was racing.

"This is Jay Theodore Masterson," I finally responded, "attorney at law. We have just received word that you are the beneficiary of a large estate left by your eminent uncle, a man who loved you like his own daughter. If you will meet me in front of the east doors of the Harold B. Smith Library in ten minutes, I will be happy to discuss the matter with you further."

Dolly said, "Erberto, is that you?" It was inevitable that Dolly perceived my deception; she always did. She sighed in her way that always sent lightning bolts through me as I heard her voice of protest from the other end of the line. "Erberto, why do you make up so many stories?"

"Maybe it isn't a story. Maybe you have a long-lost uncle that did die, leaving you millions. I think you deserve millions, Dolly."

"But I don't have any uncles that have died. That's all there is to it; I don't."

Things weren't going very well, so I decided to change tactics. I blurted out, "Dolly, you're wonderful. You're beautiful. Your eyes are like stars. You're..."

"Erberto! You read all that in a book."

"No, I didn't. It was in a movie called *For the Love of Pete*. It was a wonderful scene."

"Well," Dolly said, "I don't like it. I'd rather you didn't quote a movie at me."

"All right. You make up something better, and it better sound romantic."

"I don't want to make up anything romantic, and I don't want things to sound romantic for the sake of sounding romantic. All I want is for you to tell the truth."

Dolly was always capable of chilly rebuke. She wanted the truth. What was the truth? The truth was that I desperately loved Dolly—I just couldn't find a way to tell her. Shocked and frustrated, I noticed my hands were shaking. Sensing my failure and finding myself tongue-tied, I mumbled something about being too busy to meet for dinner anyway and ended the call. I stood weak-kneed by the phone, speechless. I was destroyed, utterly destroyed. The light of my life, the love of my heart, was gone because of my need to be clever. Ah! If I only had the power of Shakespeare's poetry or the charm of—

The phone rang again.

I picked up. "Hello?"

It was a fake, gravelly voice: "Yes, this is the Federal Fridge Inspection Bureau. Can you... uh, tell us if your stove is running?"

"You mean refrigerator?"

"Yeah. That too."

"Dolly, is that you?"

"If it is, you better go catch it!"

"Very funny." I laughed at her failed antics. "I love you for trying."

"You do?"

"Well, yeah, of course, I love you. Why else would I want you to marry me?"

"That's all you ever had to say."

Never in a Million Years

Debra Birdwell Winkler

Blind dates, matchmakers, dating websites. None are my cup of tea, shall we say. Never trusted the results of any of them. Matchmakers and dating apps take your money with little return. I had enough blind dates years ago to know they don't work out.

Oh, except for my friend, Pearl. Many years ago, after her divorce, Pearl signed up with a dating firm, and as fate would have it, she met her husband—to whom she is still married, thirty-two years and four children later. I figured I was going to be an old maid when my boss at the time introduced me to my husband, but that wasn't a blind date. He was a client, and he sat next to me at an office luncheon. Our relationship went on from there. Marriage, children, then twenty-six glorious years with him dying on our wedding anniversary. That was five sad and lonely years ago.

The last time Pearl visited me, we talked about my dating again. She'd been hounding me for the last year about it.

"Never in a million years will I find someone as special as my Ned at my age," I said to Pearl.

"You're only 65, you know. And, you are still quite a looker."

"Am not."

"Are too."

"You're just saying that because we're friends."

"No," she said. "I'm saying it because it's true."

So, she helped me sign up and even completed most of the application.

"Don't embellish," I said.

"Just trying to make you sound exciting."

"I just want to be me, okay?"

"Fine," was her reply.

Yes, I like gardening, music, the theater, hiking, and traveling. She had me change to a more appealing blouse and took a picture with her phone, along with one of me reading in my big armchair. We walked in my rose garden, and she took a couple there, choosing the one with me smelling a red rose. She added those to my profile and seemed very pleased with herself.

"Soon," she said, "you'll be getting winks and romantic letters."

"Romantic letters?" I remarked. "I'll just receive texts, that's all."

Pearl laughed. "Hey babe, we're living in a different generation than when we were young. Yesterday's romantic paper letters are today's romantic texts, although some say sexts!"

"That's not funny."

"But it's true."

It wasn't until the next day that results began to come in. Pearl sat next to me as we viewed the men who responded. Jeff in the next town over sent me a wink. Then, Peter, and two Bills. Two days later, eleven men were vying for my attention online! Pearl and I reviewed their profiles, and I discarded seven of the eleven, either because they were just not for me or lived too far away.

By the end of the month, I had met with five gentlemen for coffee. I was looking for someone I could feel comfortable with, but that didn't happen. Although each was nice, I felt apprehensive, and there was no connection, no spark.

Then, Tim sent me a wink. His profile pictures showed he was nicely dressed, had dark hair, a lovely smile, and fabulous green eyes. He was a retired history professor, which, for me as a former social studies and geography teacher, was an instant connection. One picture showed him on a beach, another biking (not my favorite past-time, but he looked very fit in that picture). The next one, he was on top of the Empire State Building and then he was at the Smithsonian. His last picture showed him at what looked like a café in Paris with some friends. I sent him a wink and, a couple of hours later, he sent me a text.

He lived in Washington, D.C., which was on the other side of the country from me. When I stated the obvious, he said he was close to retirement and looking at moving west, although he hadn't settled firmly on a location. He had been a widower for ten years. We found out we liked the same music and similar foods, enjoyed the same plays and some of the same books. And his favorite flower? You guessed it. Roses.

We could talk about anything and everything. He had traveled all over the world, speaking at conferences in Europe, the Middle East, China, Japan, South Africa, Brazil, and Australia. I'd only been to Canada and the Caribbean, but I had always wanted to visit Australia.

<I'll be in Australia at a conference the first week in January. Why don't you join me?>

<Ha,> I responded. <Can't, too much money.>

His texts were quite charming, and I was amazed how easy it was to converse with him. I kept Pearl apprised of what happened online. She wanted to know if it reminded me of those paper romantic letters I had received from my husband. As days passed, Tim was becoming more romantic. And, I must say I was experiencing a connection to him and almost feeling a bit like I was betraying Ned. Although Pearl assured me that I wasn't.

We were too far away to just meet for a cup of coffee but, a month after we met online, he said he was going to a conference in California and was going to take a four-hour layover to see me. I couldn't believe how excited I was to meet this interesting man. Pearl was thrilled for me and made suggestions of what to wear.

I waited in the coffee shop at the airport, wondering whether he would be the same person I'd gotten to know in those text messages. Was he easy-going, nice, courteous, handsome, and as fascinating as I wanted him to be?

I waited two hours. But he never showed. I felt so silly at first and then angry. No one stood me up! We only messaged through the dating app with no exchange of phone numbers or email addresses. But there was nothing from him on the app to indicate something had happened. I texted him to see if I had gotten the date wrong. Nothing. As I walked to my car, I decided I was just a foolish woman.

A week later after not hearing from him, I began to pay attention to other matches arranged for me. One guy winked at me but, when I winked back, he said New Orleans was too far away from me. I certainly agreed. I winked at several but no one local winked back. A blow to my ego, but Pearl insisted I continue.

Ten days later, DeWayne sent me a wink. He was five years older than I, had a gray crew cut, wore glasses, and had a sweet smile under that Western hat he wore. He owned a ranch in eastern Montana, describing himself as a small-town guy who loved music and played guitar in a local band in his hometown thirty miles away from his home. He was a widower who was looking for companionship and wanted to meet the last love of his life.

DeWayne was a nice guy, who after a few weeks, was growing on me. The closer I got to DeWayne, the more I began to push Tim from my mind.

Pearl suggested that I quit being so old-fashioned and give DeWayne my phone number. He immediately sent me a picture of his Montana ranch house, then he texted via phone, <Could you see yourself visiting me here on the ranch?>

<Maybe.>

<What about coming for a week or two in January?>

<Maybe.>

<I have a housekeeper and her husband who helps me around the ranch. You'll have a room all to yourself, and I'll be the perfect gentleman, I promise.>

<Maybe,> I repeated again.

<May I call you?> he texted. <I would really like to hear your voice.>

<Maybe.> Then I added a smiley face emoji.

He sent the same emoji back to me.

When I told Pearl, she said, "He seems nice enough. Why don't you go?"

"Maybe," I told her. I just didn't know if I wanted to be in the wilds of eastern Montana in the dead of winter.

The next day he called, and I was surprised De-Wayne didn't sound like he was the stereotypical hillbilly or redneck depicted on television. His voice was firm and husky, but almost sweet and tender as he said my name. I was very pleased he had called, and we talked for over an hour as he described his house and how it sat away from the road among the trees. I could almost see the entire area as he spoke. Before we hung up, he asked me to seriously think about visiting him and I said I would.

With a smile, I was tucking my phone in my pocket when my phone dinged. To my surprise, there was a message from Tim through the dating app. Tim who I should have deleted from my dating app. Tim who had so much in common with me. I ignored the message notice and turned off my phone.

After I crawled into bed that night, I looked at my phone. I read the message from DeWayne, who asked if he should go ahead and make my plane reservations. I texted, <Yes.> Then, I closed my phone, turned off the light, and settled in under the covers. I decided I'd be Scarlett O'Hara from *Gone with the Wind* and wait until tomorrow to answer Tim. After all, he had been in no rush to get back to me.

Smiling at myself, I decided I needed this little trip to Montana. DeWayne was a very nice guy, and I was lonely for companionship. And, who knew, maybe I would fall in love with the place and the man.

I was almost asleep when my phone dinged and dinged and, then, dinged again. I thought maybe something was wrong with my son or someone in his family. But no, it was just Tim. Just Tim? I had six messages from Tim. SIX! What on earth did he have to say to me when it was almost two in the morning on the east coast? I decided I needed to nip this relationship in the bud and delete Tim from my phone.

Then, I read his messages.

Text 1: <Audrey, I haven't been able to get in touch and really would like to speak with you.>

Text 2. <I have been away and unable to text you.>

Text 3: <Please talk to me so I can explain.>

Text 4: <I know it's been more than eleven weeks, but I was out of the country for work.>

Text 5: <Please forgive me for the radio silence. It was unavoidable. I have thought of you every day since the last time we texted.>

Text 6: <Audrey, please, give me something. A smile maybe?>

I ignored the messages and closed my phone, turning it off and burying it under the pillows.

I didn't sleep well and woke up with a horrid headache. I was irritated with myself for reading Tim's texts without deleting them. He remembered it had been eleven weeks, and now he thinks he can just casually text himself back into my life! How dare he? So, he needed to talk to me. So, what? *So, what indeed.*

For the next two days, I decided to ignore my phone totally.

Let him be, I told myself.

It's too late, I reminded myself.

When I did eventually turn on my phone, I remembered I had left not only Tim in the dark, but DeWayne. Two texts from DeWayne asked me to confirm my trip to Montana. I smiled as I messaged him my confirmation with no regret. He seemed to be a nice man who would take care of me.

Suddenly, DeWayne called, "Audrey, is everything okay?" His voice sounded concerned.

I answered, "Everything is great, and I am looking forward to visiting you."

"I really like you a lot, Audrey. And, you never know, you might like Montana so well you might want to stay."

"Maybe."

"Maybe you'll like me better than Montana and stay just because of me."

"You never know."

"Hey, at least it's not a *maybe*."

I laughed.

Then, he said, "I'll have the tickets delivered to you tomorrow morning, and a car will take you to the airport. I can't wait to spend New Year's Eve with you tomorrow night. Text me your address."

I sent him my address, adding, "Can't wait." I ended it with a smiley face and closed my phone.

Unexpectedly, I realized that I was ready for this meeting with DeWayne. DeWayne who lived on a ranch in eastern Montana. DeWayne who I had just conversed with on a dating app. DeWayne who was kind and caring and wanted to meet me in person. It was certainly a long way to go for a cup of coffee!

I grinned at myself, deciding that I was rather looking forward to meeting this rancher in Montana. I was really happy at this prospect.

It was almost midnight when I finally crawled into bed and plugged my phone into its charger. I wasn't going to look at Tim's messages, but curiosity got the best of me. I decided I'd read them and then delete him from my phone.

Text 1: <I remain heartbroken with no response from you.>

Text 2: <I went by your house today, but you weren't there. Please answer me. I really want to speak to you.>

Text 3: <I must sound like a stalker. I don't mean to. Please call the police if that makes you feel better. Tell them this code XX2745TT. They will let you know I am legitimate.>

I reread the texts several times. I couldn't believe he was here at my house. *How does he know where I live?* And what is this code business? Is he some confidential informant for the police or a CIA spy?

I was furious. I sat up in bed and texted him, <Who do you think you are to come to my house? I think

you really are stalking me. You disappeared into oblivion without a goodbye! I don't even know you. How did you find where I lived?>

<Thank God,> he texted. <I was worried.>

<Why?> I asked as I stood up, pacing back and forth.

<I'm going to Australia. You always wanted to visit Australia. Come join me.>

<Are you kidding?>

<No, I am very serious.>

<It's out of the question,> I said as I walked into my kitchen and pulled out a bottle of water from the fridge.

<Did you call the police and give them my code?>

I slammed the bottle of water on the counter. <I just may do that right now.>

<Go ahead, I'll wait.>

<How dare you!> I placed my phone on the counter and frantically texted. <You leave. You come back, give me a code, and expect me to travel with you? You're nuts.>

<Answer your phone.>

<It's not ringing.>

Then, the phone rang.

"Hello," I said.

"Hello, Audrey," a deep baritone voice answered. "It's Tim."

I could say nothing for a few seconds, then I demanded, "How did you get my number?"

"The same way I was able to find out your address."

"How?"

Then I was silent, trying to decide what to do. I pulled up a stool and leaned on my counter. This man who, weeks ago, I had fancied I might… could perhaps spend more time with… who I had begun to have feelings for… who just disappeared…

"Audrey? Are you there?"

I took a drink of water and was finally able to ask, "Where have you been, Tim?"

I could hear him taking a deep breath. "Just accept that I can't tell you where I was."

I laughed.

He waited and then said, "I work for the government, and I was…well on a mission, undercover, an important mission to help stop a war between two countries."

"Right. Like I'm supposed to believe that."

"Yes."

"You couldn't even say goodbye."

"No." He sighed.

"You left me waiting for you at the airport."

"I know."

"I felt like a fool. Do you understand that?"

"Yes. But I wanted to be there, to meet you. But I was called unexpectedly away. My job is like that…"

"But you were a jerk to not contact me."

"Okay, I was a jerk but not on purpose."

"Wait, I thought you were retired."

"Well, I am, sort of. I'm no longer teaching, but I still lecture at conferences just like I told you. But there are other things I do when needed."

"What things?"

"I've said too much already, Audrey."

I said nothing and let silence linger between us. Then, he said, "I want to see you, to speak to you in person, to really get to know you. More than ever. I think we're good for each other."

"I can't afford to fly to Australia on a whim."

"I'll have tickets delivered to you first thing in the morning."

"Tomorrow is New Year's Eve."

"Yes, I know. I really want to spend New Year's Eve with you so we can start a new year learning about each other and letting you know how I feel."

"But I am uncertain how I feel about you anymore."

"That's alright. We will learn more about each other and make decisions later."

I hesitated. "I don't know, Tim."

"But I do," he assured me. "A car will take you to the airport for a noon flight to Sydney."

"I just can't pick up and leave without a word to anyone. My kids would worry."

"Call your kids and tell them that you've won a free trip. Then, wait patiently for the doorbell to ring and be ready for the adventure of your life."

"But…" I began and then told him firmly, "You really hurt me with your wordless disappearance, and now you expect me to be fine flying to Australia. Heck, you might leave me at the drop of a hat over there."

"Audrey, you mean so much to me, and I want to see you. Tell you what, if I have to leave precipitously while we are there, I will have my staff arrange your flight home."

"How convenient for you to turn me over to your staff."

"Audrey, the only promise I can make is to be with you as much as possible. I don't expect to be called away for anything."

"But you were called away the last time we were supposed to meet."

"Yes, but…"

I didn't let him finish. "Tell you what," I said. "I'll think about it overnight."

"Fair enough," he said. "Just be ready when the doorbell rings." He paused and then continued, "If you decide not to come to me, tell the courier to return the tickets. No muss. No fuss. I will never contact you again."

"Okay," I said.

"Good. But know that I'm waiting for you."

I said goodbye and hung up the phone. Our conversation

had reawakened the excitement that I had originally felt for Tim.

I tossed and turned all night, trying to decide what to do as I realized how difficult the decision was going to be. No one had ever vied for my attention like these two men who had arranged to send me plane tickets to meet them and probably change my life forever.

DeWayne was the steady one with a down-to-earth lifestyle and a ranch for security. My life with him would be stable and comfortable, and he would take care of me, although maybe a little humdrum for a city girl like me.

Then, there was Tim, who was a retired professor but claimed to work in a seemingly secret position with the government and could take off into the wild blue yonder on the spur of the moment. Who knew where he lived and how chaotic my life would be with no promise of a solid foundation for a cozy, comfy life?

Which to choose? Which is more appealing? Home, home on the range or *Carpe Diem?* Safe, secure home and lifestyle, or is it time for me to just seize the day for once in my life?

It was still dark when I finally got up, but I had come to a conclusion. My brilliant thought was to allow the Fates to decide for me. Whichever set of tickets came first would confirm my destination and the man with whom I would probably spend the rest of my life.

When I looked out my kitchen window, it was snowing, and the soft opalescent light from the slow sunrise glimmered on the freezing winter wonderland. I was quite pleased with myself as I stood in my kitchen drinking coffee and nibbling on a piece of toast. I had two options, I knew that I would need warm clothes to go to Montana and, since it was summer in Sydney, I'd need suitable clothes for that climate. Therefore, I had packed two different suitcases for this adventure of mine, whichever destination it would be.

My suitcases were on either side of the front door, Montana on the left and Australia on the right. I had two coats resting on the back of my big armchair, my big heavy one with a fuzzy hood for Montana and my lighter one for Australia. Sitting on the counter next to me was my purse with my passport, I.D., and phone inside. I had just rinsed out my coffee cup and was placing it in the drainboard when the doorbell rang.

My heart was beating a mile a minute as I opened my front door to a young, well-dressed gentleman. Who knew romantic letters, disguised as texts, would lead me to this moment?

"Miss Audrey?" he asked.

I nodded. He handed me a manila envelope.

"I am to wait for you," he said.

I opened the envelope carefully and pulled out the folded papers holding my destiny. I smiled before I unfolded the papers because I knew I wouldn't have to wait a million years, after all, for love and happiness.

Then, I looked at the tickets.

What I Never Knew

Virginia Babcock

I hate being forty-five. It's especially hard being single
and childless too. All my friends and family have kids and
most are getting grandkids. Even the divorced ones. Not
me. I don't even get patronizing looks from the church
ladies anymore. Middle age doesn't suit singleness. And it
won't get any easier.

My best friend's mom told me last week that
sixty is the new forty. I look older than her. My hair
is uncolored and my body uncut. I have a few wrin-
kles, but she has none. Of course her hair can't get any
longer due to the chemistry applied to it, and her face
and boobs are stone hard and held in place with staples,
scars, and toxins.

I don't usually care about my age. I have been
successfully single all of my life. But this morning on my
way to the counter to choose three donuts for my week-

end, two men in line stare at me. I make eye contact and look away. One calls out my name, and a flash of memory provides his and the other man's—his brother's—names.

OMG! It's the boy over whom I suffered a nasty case of unrequited love as a teenager. I haven't seen him for more than twenty years. How did I recognize him? They want me to join them for breakfast. I have to see this through, but I want to blow them off.

Quickly, I excuse myself as the baker pulls my order. They agree to wait and sit at a table in the back. In the restroom, I shut myself in a stall and practice deep breathing exercises as my brain pummels me with ancient memories.

I try to process that that man who was once my teenage love didn't say my name. His older brother, whom I only met once, did. Of course, seeing one, it was easy to recognize the other; they share many genes.

X is the man I used to know. He and his brother, Y, are two in a family of eight siblings. I had been friends with X from ages sixteen through twenty-three.

I travel back to my 19-year-old self. I spent a lot of time with X, but I saw *Y* a single time, at X's missionary farewell. My little sister went with me in my second car ever: a black Firebird. I haven't thought of that car in a while.

We sat in the rear of the chapel, two strange young women attending a young man's farewell. My sister was bored and people-watched as I stared at X's friends and family, hungry for data about my crush.

Surprisingly, we were the only "groupies" who made the trek. For years, I had been the only girl in our cluster of teens who met up during regional 4-H youth activities. For most of that time, I was part of a triad. I was a young woman who became friends with a pair of young men, X and *A*, who were best friends, one of whom was a heartthrob (X) and both popular with other females.

Our group dynamic changed when we three washed up in the same engineering program at Utah State as freshmen. There I learned my triad was a horrendous love triangle, well out of my control. I wanted X. I suspected he wanted me back, but his bestie, who I could only be friends with, wanted me. In a stunted, quiet way, I began fighting the triangle. Meanwhile, A conned me into going on "pseudo dates" with him.

We should have cleared the air. I should have cut it off, and avoided both of them. They should have fought it out. Instead, they kept treating me like the tomboy I had always been.

After the farewell sacrament meeting, my sister and I joined the hordes descending on X's house. Everyone split into three groups. The immediate family, close friends, and neighbors were in the kitchen. Extended family, aunts, cousins, etc. were in the backyard where the little kids ran amok. We sat in the living room with school chums and close friends, still the only females. After shaking my hand, X shook my sister's and then disappeared into the clutches of his mother and aunties. I didn't see him again until after his mission.

I felt a bit out of place there. I knew many of the college friends, but none of the locals. A was on his own mission already. Having been greeted and abandoned by X, I was making small talk and keeping my sister comfortable. I was contemplating leaving when Y appeared to "entertain" the front room. He sat next to me and changed the atmosphere. Like a good host, he got us conversing more naturally and stood in well for his brother.

Adrenaline has corrupted the rest of my memory. I know I talked with everyone, and my sister and I had a good time. We chatted happily the whole way home. I plotted whether I could finally break through my love triangle. I hoped the two years of separation while X and A were on their missions would help.

I exit the ladies room in the donut shop and go straight to the pick-up counter. A baker hands me my box. I concentrate on not tripping as I make my way to the brothers' table.

I can't help but stare at the brothers. Years ago, I was struck by how much they looked alike, except X had creamy ivory skin like new wood, dark brown hair like espresso, and medium blue eyes like my favorite denim jeans before they fade to soft sky blue. His older brother had the same face, body, and hairline, but his skin was like clear-coated oak with warm brown hair the color of a grizzly bear's fur and hazel eyes.

But time had changed them. X still has a full head of hair like their mother, but now Y is bald like their dad. They aged well. Skin darkened to a yummy weathered brown, few gray hairs, no paunch, and strong vigor in their movements. X still looks good. He should be married. I don't know any details about Y.

Much drama happened to our triad, but the gist is the two guys served two missions, A came home from his mission early after an auto accident, and I got the job that became my real job, but it was in another city.

Eventually, A took me to see Star Wars. I sat in my red Trans Am, when A called to say his clingy roommate was joining us. As they arrived, X stared at me from the back seat of the Suburban. The whole night became a tug-of-war between two guys.

We all had a lot of fun, despite some posturing and testosterone poisoning. I gave up trying to have a meaningful conversation with them. X flirted with me the whole time before feigning sleep on the way home. That's how I learned he didn't really want me. I was just a toy for them to fight over.

All this left me heartsore, so I cut ties with them. Here we sit more than twenty years later. I truly cut ties, I never even cyber stalked X or A on Google, or Facebook when it became popular. I feel awkward as hell, but the conversation flows as easily as it ever did.

I always wondered whether I would survive meeting my teenage crush. I feel stronger than expected. As we eat, I notice neither is wearing a wedding ring.

"Did you hear what happened with A?" X asks.

I shrug. "No. When I last saw him he was really depressed. When he learned how much I was making, he never called me again. I know he dropped out of school and quit working. He was living in his grandma's basement."

"Yeah. You know how the car accident messed up his head?"

"Yes. It was a TBI, right?"

"Yes. When his last girlfriend left him and married another guy, he lost it. A psychic break. He was in and out of treatment for a year. And after, he was mostly a wreck. He's been back home with his parents ever since," X said.

"Man, that's too bad."

"Didn't you and A have a thing?" Y interjects.

"Nope. Not really."

"But you were always hanging out with him. Every time I saw you picking up X, you were with A already," Y says.

I don't know what to say. I go with the truth, "Well. He wanted to, but he never actually asked me on a date."

"Never?" X asks.

"What can I say? I was hanging out. If he wanted more, he should have said or done something," I say.

"But he was such a player with the younger gals. He always said he was just killing time with them until you came around," X says.

"He never even tried to kiss me, let alone hold my hand. We may have hugged, but as friends only," I say.

"I never knew," X says.

After patting X on the back, Y says, "Told you. You should have asked her."

"Ask me what?"

"Whether you were one of A's harem. All the other guys in their group said you were his queen bee. And he warned X to stay away from you," Y says.

I laugh hysterically. This continues for nearly a minute. Tears are starting when I finally regain control. "Holy shit. I knew you two had a bros agreement. Why the hell didn't either of you ask me what I wanted? Dammit." I stand. Exorcising baggage is a good thing, cleansing even, but it is NOT comfortable, especially around strangers and in public.

"Wait. Where are you going?" X says.

"Somewhere else. That was a long time ago and far away." I shake my head. "All I ever wanted back then was a chance with you. I even took you to my house to see my mom, to show you more about me, to see if it could work. I don't need to know what I suspected all along is true. It doesn't matter now, anyway. Neither one of you had the balls to talk to me about this, so we were always 'friends.'"

"I suspected, but..." X says.

I cut him off. "But, nothing. Last I heard you were married. Besides, when I asked God, He told me you weren't the one for me. That finally healed the heart of the teenage girl I used to be."

X is gobsmacked. "That's fair. We were friends though, right?"

"Unfortunately, or fortunately yes," I say.

"You were the only woman that was genuine with me at that time."

"Thank you. That's how I roll."

I leave. Somehow I reach my truck. I get in, stash the donut box, and put on my seatbelt. I hold the steering wheel with two hands. This is not the way I had planned to spend my Saturday morning.

As I ponder, Y taps his finger on my window. He holds up a smartphone. I push the start button and roll down the window.

"I know it's not a good time right now, but will you share your number with me? I've always heard positive things about you, and he's reeling over this too. We may want to get together with you sometime in the future. He was sure you were A's girl. I think you blew his mind," Y says.

"Well. Too late is too late, but here's my number," I say.

Y sends me a text with his number and another with X's. He thumps my door with his hand. "Regardless of any discomfort, it was good to see you today. I haven't thought back to college in a while. It was good to reminisce. Drive safe."

I say something like "understand" and "you too," but my mind is still a blur to focus. I buck up just enough to drive safely. At home the only things I accomplish are parking the truck in the garage and eventually eating my other two donuts. "What ifs" are awful, messy thoughts, and I am overwhelmed by them.

Sunday morning arrives. I wake in a stupor at five AM. Tylenol PM enabled me to get a few hours of shut-eye, but you can't tell by looking at me. Dark circles and bedhead hair do not make a middle-aged female look younger. I pop my vitamins and chug a bottle of water as I contemplate how ready to be today. Deciding that even a bra is too much work, I lie back down in bed.

Before I know it, I'm sleeping. At nine-thirty, I roll over. I need the toilet. I'm also missing church. I stagger into the bathroom. I'm still in a dream as I wash my hands. I look in the mirror, but see images in my mind.

I'm back on the day of X's farewell. The dream leaves me with three new impressions. First, Y was flirting with me the whole time I was at their house. He was talking to everyone but his eyes were on me. I recall my sister saying something about that, but I brushed it off. Secondly, I remember shaking Y's hand. It was warm and firm and he lingered. Finally, Y really did ask to take a ride with us in my Firebird. While I was making eyes at X, Y was making eyes at me. *Holy cow!*

I can't take it. Learning that I could have had a chance with either X or Y when I was young is too much. I collapse on the bathroom floor. Why am I thinking about this now?

My phone chimes with a text. I crawl fifteen feet to my bedside table to read from Y, <I know it's the Sabbath, but can I take you to breakfast? I'd like to talk with you.> *OMG. Is this really happening? Is this a sign?* The dream is controlling me. Is a buried subconscious longing for someone to love causing me to imagine all this?

Instinct or inspiration makes me reply, <Yes. I already missed church. When? Where? I'll meet you.>

He types, <Is 10:30 too soon?> and names my favorite diner.

I measure the state of my laundry in my head and look at the clock. Forty-five minutes, a shower, and an outfit, I can make it. I type, <Yes. Meet you there.>

His answer is speedy. <I'll watch for your truck. I'll be inside or in my blue Chevy. It's a few years older than yours.>

I shower. My hair stays dry and gets braided, then brushed out into its usual poof. Clean teeth and moistur-ized face finish the regimen as I dither over which ear-rings. I wear my best jeans and my warm winter boots. A puffer jacket, my wallet, phone, and key fob, and I am out the door.

As I go, I feel the same excitement I've always felt before a hopeful date. But this is based on assumptions. Y is probably married and has some sort of bombshell to drop on me.

I hear voices in my mind. I think of one of my dear friends who lives with schizophrenia, and consider that I could be losing it. But the chorus in my head seems friendly and benevolent if a bit pushy. They are repeating, *Go now. Get there.*

The Sunday brunch herd half-fills the parking lot. I see a few trucks, but only one blue Chevy. I park my gray Chevy next to it. Y is not in the truck. I head into the diner.

Y, and only Y, is sitting near the hostess station. He stands as I enter. "Thank you for coming on short notice. I have a few things I wanted… I mean, I wanted to talk with you, and couldn't wait."

I fight being flustered. "You have my full attention."

The hostess steps forward. She holds two menus. Y is right behind me as we follow her. He pulls out my chair and sits after I do.

I open my menu for something to do as I decide which of my favorites to order. Y doesn't open his; he looks at me instead.

I ask, "What? You're making me nervous. Say what you need to say."

He smiles. "Great. I will. First, being a 47-year-old, single guy, I just can't wait any longer."

That sounds creepy to me. "What do you mean?"

He seems to realize what he's said. "Oh no. I don't think that came out right. I just... well, you know... I mean you ran out so fast yesterday. Seeing you out of the blue like that with X, I was shocked to see you, and wanted to talk more."

I'm feeling a bit leery, but the chorus in my head is still chirping at me. "Okay. So?"

"It's just that I never got that ride in your Firebird."

"My Firebird? You mean at X's farewell?"

He nods. "I was so hoping for that ride. Um, like X, I should have said something at the time." He takes a breath. "I had seen you a few times and heard a lot about you. From X, from Z, even Mom and Dad. But I never got the chance to meet you until that day, and you were so into X, that you hardly saw me."

"Sorry about that. Now you know where I was." I tap my temple.

"Yes, but I'd like you to know where I was." He points to the side of his head. "I never got the chance to get to know you then, but I wanted to. Would you be willing to get to know me now?"

"Are you asking me out?"

"Yes, if you are willing. I know you were fun, smart, and interesting. And now, I know you were more into my brother than A; that gives me hope."

"Wow. You move fast."

"Oh, sorry. Let me say it this way. I am single and relatively unencumbered. I liked your look then; I like it now. Everything I've ever heard about you intrigued me. And you are fun to talk to. Can we call this," his hand circles the table, "a first date, almost like a blind date?"

I need more data, and it's been a while since I dated anyone. "I've always had a policy to go on at least one date."

"Good." He reaches across the table to pat my hand, "If it's any inducement, I am a lot funnier and smarter than my brother, though he kept our hair." He makes a swipe at the thick locks above his ear. He looks me over again. "But, you're back to your great coiffure. I was shocked to see it so short at X's farewell."

I blurt, "Well, you, like your dad, have a nice head to pull it off." I pause, his observation shocked me. "You saw it before I cut it?"

"Yes. With our dad being an Extension agent, do you think any of us kids weren't in 4-H? I saw you for the first time the summer X turned sixteen. You went on that weeklong trip to the Shakespeare Festival. For days after you should have heard X complain that both you and A had your drivers licenses already and he had to wait. I also heard about your hair at the winter retreat."

"Oh no. Not the spin the bottle game!"

"Yes! X said he was aiming for your cheek, but you ducked and he got a mouthful of those locks."

I covered my face with my hands, transported back to the long ago day where at sixteen, the winter before the Shakespeare trip, when I'd met A and X for the second time in our lives, and played my first game of spin the bottle. On my turn, I dropped my head and barely felt X swooping in. I have a lot of long, naturally curly, coarse hair. I'd worn it long all my life before getting it cut to just above my ears right after high school.

Y gently pulls one hand off my face. "Hey, you okay in there?"

I shake my head. "No. That was nearly thirty years ago, and my first and only game of spin the bottle." I know my face is red.

He smiles, "Believe me. I understand. You should know, I used to pump X for information about you. I know all the dirt. Besides the infamous date where A and X were fighting over you at Star Wars and your red Firebird that X got to ride in, but again, I didn't, I know about the 4-H State Contests at USU where you face-planted in that killer dress."

I cringe. My hand moves back over my face. I squeak out, "The dress?"

"Yes, the velvety long thing that, and I'm sorry to quote, 'showed off your 'assets' and made you look hot.' X said the best thing about it was after you fell walking up to your seat in the nosebleed section, you were pink and embarrassed but laughed harder than any of the guys with you. A few minutes later, you went on stage to get your award looking poised and confident."

"Again, I was sixteen, and I try to forget that ever happened."

"That's why I want to know you." Y nabs both my hands, pulls them down to the table, and holds them within his. "You kept going. You were also true. Few kids are true at that age. Any female who looks so good, keeps up with the boys in jokes and brains, and drives like a secret service agent, is definitely worth knowing. I suspect she still exists and has only gotten better with age."

I gulp. I don't hold hands, but his feel nice, so I let him keep mine.

He persists. "While I was on my mission, I only heard pieces of what you and X did when you were seventeen and eighteen, but I did hear that you know all the words to 'The Scotsman' song and sing it on demand."

"Heavens. He told you about that?"

"Yes. He said while you all were walking to a chem lab, A asked to borrow your Dr. Demento mix tapes so he could learn the words, and one of the other guys dared you to sing it. You did. All verses and in tune."

"Sigh."

"You intimated the heck out of my little brother. The word 'scary' was used."

I shake my head. "Well I'm getting paid back now."

That makes him laugh.

His thumbs stroke the back of my hands. They are warm and firm like they were in my dream, and nicely, a little rough.

I think of Mom. She's long given up on me having kids, and worries that I'll die alone. She tells me things like "give any guy who is interested a chance" and to "pick the right brother." Here is a guy, possibly the right brother, that knows some of my most embarrassing teenage moments and isn't put off.

I stare at him. He stares back at me. He's still handsome, and more so than even X at nineteen due to his greater self-assurance. With his quirky smile I notice a dimple. Damn. I go through my short list of dealbreakers. He's taller than me; speaks up for himself; has no trouble with me driving a truck, and has a real job.

He speaks, "I see you plotting in that head of yours. FYI, I've never been married. School and work kept me too busy and frankly too poor for a wife when I was younger, and by the time I was thirty-five, I could never find the right woman. Too old or too young, or too many kids."

I can't help but reply. "Well I've never married either, and no babies, and no chance of them."

"That's no problem with me. Being one of eight, and at my age, I'm okay with no babies. I've never figured I'd get married, and accordingly never figured on having kids." He pauses. "Whoa. Sorry, I didn't mean to imply that we should get married. I mean, my long-term goal, if I were to find the right woman, would be marriage, but right now, I'd just like to get to know you for real, for myself."

I feel like smiling and do. "That works for me too."

The Return to Cherry Hill

Elizabeth Suggs

"You came," Presley said without looking up from her ale. She kept her eyes on the foam, how it rocked back and forth with her hand's movements. It was the only way she could keep her eyes off of him. If she stopped rocking her cup— stopped watching the foam—then maybe she'd see the hurt carved into Elias' face. She couldn't deal with that, just as much as she couldn't deal with him before it all happened.

"Of course I came," Elias said.

His voice was deeper than she remembered, but then again, it had been nearly a year since they were in the same room together. Her memory had never been perfect—she must have imagined parts of him to make it easier to stay away. Her ill dad had needed her more than her heart needed love, but now look at her. She couldn't save her dad, and somehow she wound up back in her old city waiting to meet her ex-boyfriend.

"It's good to see you," he said, sliding into the booth across from her. His southern Welsh accent was just as thick as she remembered. It felt good to hear it again.

She raised her head slightly to see him holding the same amber beer as her. They had always enjoyed the same drink. Did he still love his coffee just as strong and bitter? And his cookies a little too sweet? She wanted to reach out to him, hold him in her arms, but she held herself still.

"It's good to see you too," Presley said, not sure if she really believed her words. This was supposed to be a happy reunion, but her thoughts kept taking her back to that last meeting on their special hill. It seemed like a million years ago.

As she wiped the foam from her mouth, she finally dared herself to look up at his face. He was scruffier than she remembered, which highlighted his angled jaw. And his muscles. Had he been working out? Or was that how he had always looked?

Their eyes locked, causing her heart to leap in her chest. For the lack of anything to say, she swallowed thick gulps of her frosty ale, allowing the alcohol to burn down her throat until her glass was empty.

"Need another drink?" he asked, jumping up from his seat a little too quickly. He bumped his head on the pendant light above the table, but he pretended to be unphased. He grabbed her glass, and for the briefest of moments, their fingers touched. His hand was warm compared to hers, rekindling a piece of her long forgotten.

"Yes," she said softly. The simple word she had wanted to say before, but couldn't. She hadn't been ready to start a family then, not when her father had needed her. She had let herself believe their hill was a fairytale—that they would never work. Yet, now, looking into his bright green eyes, "yes" meant more than he understood.

She had hoped tonight would be their night, but then, a woman at the bar, with long legs and straight black hair exclaimed, "Elias! How are you?" She touched his shoulder, lingering just a little too long and laughing a little too loudly at something he said.

When he returned, Presley dropped her eyes to her hands. She fought a rising blush to her cheeks as a beer was set in front of her.

"I'm sorry about your dad," he said softly. "Nobody knew how to wrack up deductions like him. I'll miss him helping me on my taxes."

Presley cocked a smile. "My dad really loved you like a—" She paused and bit back the last word. "Anyway, he's at peace now."

"Remember when the three of us had a picnic on Cherry Hill?"

Presley smiled. "Oh, yeah, and the ants got into my dad's surprise birthday cake?"

"It really was a surprise, wasn't it?"

"I will never live down that first bite!" Presley said.

Elias nodded and raised his drink. "To Walter Campbell! And renewed friendships!" he said and banged his glass against hers, accidentally spilling her beer onto her lap.

"I'm so sorry!" His accent curved thick around her body, soaking her more than the pooling alcohol.

"It's alright," she said, clearing her throat and left for the bathroom.

Presley walked up to the bathroom sink and stared at her reflection. She couldn't help but smile at his clumsiness. His embarrassment was even more endearing than she remembered.

Dried off, she exited the restroom and saw the same raven-haired woman, now at their table, in her seat, leaning close to Elias' face.

"I'll see you Saturday night, right?"

Elias looked up, dumbstruck, face crimson, as if caught in the act.

Presley rushed out of the bar with tears in her eyes. Was she a fool to think a second chance at love was possible?

"Presley!" he called out.

She sped to her car and fled the scene. A thousand thoughts raced through her mind. Without forethought, she found herself in a familiar location. She followed the bike trail that they had ridden countless times up to their hill.

In the fall, the foliage was an explosion of orange and red. In winter, the hill was a twinkling mound of ivory. But now it was spring—her favorite. That's when the cherry blossoms bloomed, and nothing was more glorious.

She collapsed at the top of the hill and wept. She remembered how simple things used to be. How they would stare up at the clouds and create stories of their life, like the sky interpreted their future.

"Hey, that cloud looks like the home I've always pictured us having," Elias said, joining her on the grass. His musk tickled her nostrils, and memories flooded of their time together.

She sucked in her breath and looked up at him. "What are you doing here?"

"I come here sometimes when I'm feeling nostalgic and homesick. I'm happy you're here, though." He took her hand in his.

She furrowed her brow. "But what about your date Saturday?

Elias frowned. "You mean my date with spin class? I go every week. I wanted to introduce you to the instructor and invite you to join me, but you ran out before I had a chance. She came over to help clean my mess, and she had this for you." He handed her a coupon for a free class. "I'd like you to come."

She locked gazes with him, falling into his dark green eyes, a sea from another world. He reached out his hand, stroking her cheek.

"Do you think that cloud is big enough for two kids?" She gestured up to a large cloud in the sky.

Elias smiled and answered with a kiss.

Sweet as Whiskey

Sara Wetmore

"So, you have a date?" Jack asked.

Sam took a long sip of her beer, the cool bubbles bursting on her tongue as she held back the words she wanted to speak behind closed lips.

"Yes, I suppose I do," she said, faking a smile.

She stared longingly at Jack, though she tried to disguise it, even as the memory of what he had looked like without his shirt, how he had tattoos on his torso as well as his arms, made her skin tingle. She rubbed her forearm quickly to rid herself of goosebumps.

There could be no evidence that she still liked him. Not in front of her coworkers. She was grateful for the time that she got to spend with him, even if he had broken things off. He was always so kind to her, ever since she started at the digital marketing agency eight months prior. When no one would talk to her, he invited her out to lunch with a group of other coworkers. And when she was feel-ing stressed, he was always there to lend an ear. Perhaps that's why they clicked in the first place. But she had to be careful. Jack always insisted that their previous fling had to remain secret. Her coworkers were all very perceptive, especially Gabe. If they found out her secret crush, they would tell him, and then Sam would certainly be hurt again.

"Who are you going on a date with?" Gabe asked.

Sam had to think about this for a moment. She didn't want to admit she had found a date on Tinder be-cause doing so would be to admit that she herself was on Tinder. She was afraid it seemed desperate.

"His name is Will. My friend set me up on a blind date," she lied, twisting her pint of beer in her hands.

"What does he look like?" Jack said curiously.

"I don't really know," Sam lied again. She had seen a picture of Will holding up a fish on his profile. She had broken her Tinder rule of never meeting up with a man with a fishing picture or gym selfie. Maybe because he seemed nice. Maybe because she was desperate, after all.

"Oh!" Gabe shouted over the din of the pub. "So, you've never seen his face?"

Sam took another long slurp of beer, licking the foam off her upper lip.

"Afraid not," she said. "There's really nothing to tell. We're meeting at the fancy pizza place down the street in fifteen minutes. And you better not follow me!" Sam nudged Gabe hard with her elbow. But as she nudged him, she locked eyes with Jack across the table.

"What if it's a disaster? Do you have a plan to get out of it?" asked Lauren, Sam's boss.

"You could always text me if you need an excuse to leave," Jack chimed in.

Sam felt the goosebumps return.

"We'll see how it goes," she said. "I may take you up on that."

Gabe left and returned with a round of tequila shots for the table. He hesitated as he handed Sam her shot glass.

"Some liquid courage," he said. "You got this."

Sam pulled the glass from Gabe's fingers, lifted it to her mouth, and slammed it back, gasping a little after she swallowed. She eyed her pint of beer before glancing at the clock on her phone. It was time to leave. She thought about asking if anyone wanted to finish her beer for her, but when she thought about Will holding up a trout, she reconsidered and quickly chugged the remaining golden liquid from her glass.

"Okay, I'm out of here. Wish me luck," Sam said, gathering her things.

Lauren rose from her seat and gave Sam a hug goodbye, and suddenly the rest of her coworkers did the same. All except Jack. Sam looked at him briefly, trying to read him, and as she approached for a hug, he extended his arm and shook her hand. His intentions could not be more clear.

Sam left the pub, looking back at Jack, who was laughing among their colleagues. She wished she could stay in his company, but the warmth from his handshake goodbye reminded her that she'd have better luck trying to date someone who was actually interested in her. Someone, perhaps, like Will.

Sam scowled to discover she was the first to arrive at the restaurant. Nothing irked her more than tardiness. She pondered this a moment. It wasn't too late to leave, to blow off the date altogether. She could walk one block north and join her coworkers once again. But then she'd have to explain what happened. The only thing worse than lying about a blind date would be chickening out before the date ever happened.

Suddenly, Sam felt a tap on her shoulder. She recognized the face, though he was shorter than he looked on his profile. Sam wished she had worn flats instead of heels to work that day.

"Sam?" the man asked.

She quickly swept her midnight hair out of her face. "Yes, hi," Sam's voice quivered, "You must be Will."

"Yes!" he said enthusiastically, moving in for a hug.

This startled Sam, and she slowly wrapped one arm around him, careful not to let their bodies touch.

She felt more comfortable once they had been seated at a table in the corner, an emergency exit sign hovering above Will's head.

"So," Will said, trying to fill the silence. "What do you do?"

"I'm a software tester," Sam said, staring more at the hostess filling up her water glass than at the date in front of her. "What about you?"

"Oh, cool. Me? I'm a musician."

Great, Sam thought, *guess I'm paying for dinner*.

She knew it was polite to ask about his music, but she had little interest in hearing about it. She dated no one but bass players as a teenager. The idea of dating another self-professed musician lost its luster years ago. She could tell Will was waiting for her to ask about his so-called job, but she decided not to ask. He scrambled to keep the conversation moving.

"Can I get a glass of the Merlot?" Sam asked, flagging down a waiter.

"Sure," the waiter said. "And you, sir?"

"Just water. Thanks," Will mumbled.

This seemed peculiar to Sam. So strange, in fact, that despite polite decorum, she decided to investigate.

"Surely you don't expect me to drink all by myself?" she said.

Will raised the sleeve of his button-up, displaying a series of roman numerals, indicating a date in thick black ink. "Three years clean."

"Ah. More for me, then," Sam said, taking a few long sips of wine. It was ten minutes into her date, and her glass was nearly empty.

A silence fell upon the table and Sam and Will looked around the restaurant, searching for something to fill the space between them. Finally, a waiter interrupted them to take their orders.

"Want to share a cap… capriccosa… pizza " he stumbled over his words.

"It's pronounced cap-reach-ee-osa," Sam corrected, "And I can't. It's got prosciutto on it."

"Oh, are you Jewish?" he said.

"No, I'm vegetarian," Sam corrected him once more. It was getting annoying having to amend his speech so frequently. "Besides, I'm starving. I'll have a margherita pizza, please," she said, addressing the waiter.

Will sighed and ordered the capricciosa for himself.

Sam didn't care that she was being rude. She wished she was sitting there with Jack instead, like they used to. At least they got along. They could talk about video games and their personal *Game of Thrones* predictions like they did in stolen moments together. There wouldn't be this painful distance between them. Things would be delightfully normal.

"So, I gather you like fishing?" Sam finally said, shedding her disappointment and trying for once to be polite.

"Not really," Will retorted.

"But in your picture, you're holding up a fish?"

"That was just one time when I was on vacation. I don't really fish."

Sam had no response to this.

After a time, she rose from her seat and said softly, "Can you excuse me? I just need to use the restroom." Instinctively, she grabbed her purse. She thought about leaving the restaurant altogether, but couldn't bring herself to stick Will with the check and no explanation. Instead, she stood outside the women's bathroom and began writing a text to Jack.

<Date is a disaster. Are you still at the pub?> She tapped send.

She waited impatiently for a reply, but as she stood there awkwardly outside the bathroom doors, nothing. Not wanting to return to the table to wait for their food with Will, Sam decided to use the restroom to take up extra time. As she was washing her hands, she felt a vibration in her purse.

Clumsily, she withdrew her phone and gazed at the screen with relief.

<No, at my friend Scott's place. Want to come?> Jack had replied.

<YES!!!> Sam wrote desperately. <Address?>

And then she stuffed her phone back in her bag, happy to have found an escape from her date.

When she returned to the table, Will was stuffing his face with pizza while her own was sitting there getting cold. Sam didn't mind. She draped her bag over the back-rest of her seat and began munching away at her margherita pizza, leaving the mangled crusts on her plate.

Sam and Will ate in silence, which was probably for the best, Sam decided. As soon as she was finished eating, she flagged down a waiter for the check and, in a courteous act that surprised even herself, picked up the tab for both herself and Will.

"This was fun," Will said with a forced cheerfulness, but his sullen face seemed to suggest otherwise.

They rose from their seats. "Want to go grab some coffee or something?"

"I can't," Sam said. "My friend is expecting me." Will leaned in for a hug goodbye. "I'll call you sometime?"

"Sure," she said curtly.

Sam wrapped one arm around his gaunt frame, feeling sick from the lies they were telling each other. If only he knew that she was really going to meet the man she had been thinking of all night, the man she really liked.

Still, despite the horrendously awkward date, Sam was feeling chipper as she walked to her car. She decided it would be a nice gesture to pick up a pack of beer on her way to Jack's friend's apartment.

At the gas station, Sam worried over which beer would be the most impressive to Jack. Surely not just a pack of Coors, and Stella Artois would seem like she was trying too hard. Besides, did anyone actually drink Stella Artois? Ultimately, she settled on a twelve-pack from a local brewery that contained a mix of amber ale, IPA, and porter beers. While she didn't know Jack exceptionally well, there had to be something in there that he liked.

Finally, Sam pulled up to the apartment and knocked on the door. Jack answered as the sound of video game combat echoed through the doorway.

"Hi," Sam said sheepishly, brushing her dark hair behind her ear, avoiding eye contact.

"Hey!" Jack exclaimed, "Come on in. We're just playing some *Diablo 3*. Oh, you brought beer! Cool, thanks."

Sam walked into the living room where a short blond man with a pirate's beard sat on the couch, leaning intently towards the TV as his fingers tripped over toggles and buttons on a Playstation controller.

"This is my friend, Scott," Jack said. "Scott, this is my coworker, Sam."

Sam winced. She hated being introduced as his coworker. Not only did this confirm that they weren't even friends anymore, but that the chances of them ever dating again (even in secret) were slim to none.

"Hey!" Scott chirped, looking back briefly from his game. "Want to play some *Diablo*?"

"No, thanks. I'm fine just watching," Sam said, taking a seat on the opposite end of the couch. She withdrew a dark beer from the box she brought and cracked it open, letting out a small hiss and the bubbling sound of rising foam.

"So, how was the blind date?" Jack laughed.

Sam was dreading this question.

"Well, for starters, he has no real job, unless you count being a musician a real job, and I picked up the bill—though I admit, he didn't expect me to. I just felt bad for him." Sam could feel her face getting red.

Jack and Scott laughed heartily.

"It wasn't really a blind date, was it?" Jack pressed.

"No," Sam confessed, "It was a Tinder date." She hung her head in shame.

"I've had a few bad Tinder dates," Scott said, glancing at her bright red cheeks. "Dating is so hard."

Sam waited to see if Jack had anything to say on the matter, but he remained silent and stoic as he poured himself a shot of Seagrams 7 Whiskey on the coffee table.

"Want a shot?" he offered Sam. But she wiggled her beer can, which was still nearly full, and said, "No, I have to drive."

Jack shrugged and downed the shot before picking up a video game controller and engrossing himself in a game of *Diablo*.

"I'm glad you wisened up and decided to come hang here," Jack said after a moment.

Sam's heart lightened. "Yeah, me too."

Jack smiled at her, and for a few minutes, her stomach twisted, and her heart palpitated. He used to smile at her all the time, but that stopped months ago. Or perhaps she'd been too distracted to notice.

"I'm going out for a smoke," Scott said, rising from the couch and putting on his jacket.

"I could go for a smoke," Sam replied, though she wasn't a habitual smoker. Just a casual one, when she was stressed or at parties. "It's been a long evening."

"Well, put on your coat and let's go," Scott said hastily. So, Sam put on her coat and followed him onto the balcony, leaving Jack to play video games by himself.

Scott pulled two cigarettes out of the pack in his pocket, handing one gingerly to Sam. She placed it in between her red lips, and Scott lit it for her. For a moment, she wondered if she was attracted to Scott, but as she stood a few inches above him, even with her heels removed, she decided against it. Besides, she had dug herself in deep with Jack. Sometimes, she tried to refill her cup of coffee around the same time that Jack arrived in the office in the morning just to ask in passing how he was doing. She was utterly, deeply obsessed.

"So you like Jack, huh?" Scott asked bluntly.

Sam gasped. "How did you know?"

"I could tell the moment you walked in," he said, "That, and Jack might have told me you used to have a thing."

"Oh no," Sam clapped her hand to her forehead in dismay, "You don't suppose he knows I still like him, right!?"

Scott took a long drag off his cigarette.

"This is a disaster," Sam said, "I don't think I can bear to go back in there."

"Don't be so hard on yourself," Scott laughed, "He still likes you, too."

"He does?" Sam gaped.

"Yes, but I wouldn't get your hopes up. He said he doesn't date coworkers."

There it was. The reason he broke things off. All of the sneaking around became too much for him. It appeared that he hadn't changed his mind about that, even if his feelings for her remained.

Sam sighed, "It's not fair, is it? The ones you want to be with can never be with you."

Scott blew a plume of smoke, words of wisdom following them into the autumn night air, "Love stinks."

"I'll drink to that." Sam snuffed out her cigarette.

Scott opened the door for her, and she followed him inside. She couldn't wait to return to her beer, but as she approached the couch, Jack patted the seat next to him, beckoning her to sit down. Things were different now that Scott had told his secret. Sam couldn't bear knowing how things could be, and yet, how they would never be at the same time.

"You know, I think I will have that shot now after all," she said, scooching towards the coffee table.

Jack paused the game and set down the controller. They both reached for the whiskey bottle simultaneously, his fingers grazing Sam's ever so lightly. Embarrassed, Sam retrieved her hand while Jack poured her a shot of amber liquid. As he twisted the cap back on, Sam held the hand he touched close to her face, thinking that was the most intimate they had been since their summer tryst.

Jack scooted the brimming shot glass over toward Sam. She waited for him to retract his hand before she reached for it and slammed it back, twisting her face as she swallowed.

"This is awful," she chuckled, coughing a little into her sleeve.

"Yeah, it's cheap whiskey, but it gets the job done," he laughed.

Sam watched for the next several hours as Jack and Scott descended farther and farther into hell in *Diablo 3*. When she looked at the time next it was one o'clock in the morning. She stretched her limbs up toward the dimly lit bulb on the ceiling and let out a deep yawn.

"I think I'd better get going." Sam rose from the couch and grasped the strap of her purse.

Jack stood up with her. "Thanks for coming. Let me walk you out."

Sam's cheeks bloomed bright red. "Thank you for saving me from my date."

Jack shrugged, as if it were no big deal.

"It was nice meeting you!" Scott called as they exited the room. Sam and Jack walked close together as they approached the door of the apartment.

Sam called out the same words to Scott awkwardly over her shoulder, catching glimpses of Jack's tattooed, tall body following close behind her.

Finally, they reached the door, and she turned around to say goodbye to Jack, but before she could meet his gaze, before she could even blink, Jack wrapped his arm behind her, placing his strong hands on the small of her back, pulling her into a kiss. Sam was too surprised to kiss him back, though he tasted sweet as whiskey.

Jack pulled back, and they stared at each other for a brief moment.

"I thought you didn't date coworkers," she said, catching her stolen breath.

Jack caressed her cheek. "You seem worth the risk."

Hearing these words, Sam gripped his head, greeting her lips to his and savoring the touch of his hands grasping her hips.

Her evening had been rescued after all.

This Dance

Austin Slade Perry

The ballet studio buzzed with jittery 20-somethings haphazardly warming up while socializing. I propped my leg up on the barre and stretched. The dancers nearby, unfazed by my entrance, continued their conversation.

"I heard he once performed on stage with a live bear!" Bethany said.

"That's ridiculous," James scoffed.

"I heard his mother started teaching him ballet the moment he started walking," Samantha said.

I rolled my eyes and ignored their gossip about the mysterious new prodigy. I looked up into the mirror; my dark hair hung in loose curls over my gray eyes.

"Emmett Price!" The artistic director of the company, Camilla, was an older woman with dark skin and silver curly hair. She was so small that when she came up and gave me a hug the top of her head barely hit my chest.

"Good morning," I smiled.

"Are you ready for the new season?" she asked.

"Always am!"

"I heard from a little mouse that you worked with a dancing coach over the break." A sly smile crept across her face.

I nodded. Word travels fast in the ballet community.

"Makes me wonder what aspirations you might have for the new season?" she continued.

I glanced around the room. My stomach tightened. Most of the dancers had been dancing since they were eight; whereas, I had to beg my parents to start dancing when I was twelve. I could see how talented my peers were, and I always felt behind. I wanted to pursue bigger roles. Truly I did. It had been a dream, but was I ready?

"We'll see what happens," I said.

She placed her hand on my shoulder and lowered her voice, "Emmett, I've seen what you can do. You have some real talent; please don't waste it." She patted my shoulder, then turned to the room, "Attention, everyone!" The dancers went silent. "There have been some rumors about a new member joining the company. Well, I am happy to say they are true. May I introduce, Sergei Alekseyev!"

A lean man with short blonde hair emerged from Camilla's office. He was tall, about a half-foot taller than me, with fair skin. He wore black tights and a long jacket, unzipped enough to expose his muscular chest. There was something very familiar about him, but I couldn't place it.

"Sergei has come to New York City from the Vaganova Academy of Ballet. We had the privilege of watching him perform last season and offered him a spot in our company," Camilla explained. "Sergei, would like to give us a demonstration of what they teach their dancers in Russia?"

He nodded and peeled off his jacket as a remix of Chopin played. He moved with ease across the floor.

His style of dancing, a combination of graceful ballet and improvised contemporary, intensified the familiar feeling tugging at my brain.

Who are you?

The music picked up, and he matched with growing intensity. Sergei dropped to his knees, lifting and lowering one knee at a time as he spun in time with the music.

That's it! His signature move.

The memories of dance school flooded back to me. I was fifteen when a new student joined our class. His family had moved temporarily for work, so we only attended school together for a semester. I was so intimidated by his prowess that I avoided him, but he was always around, watching me practice.

The song climaxed, and he leaped, landing inches in front of me with expert precision.

Heat radiated off of him, filling the air between us. A roar of applause sang out from the group as he lifted his head.

"Hello, Emmett," he said in a hushed voice.

"Thank you for that demonstration," Camille said. "We have a lot of work to do before the spring showcase next month, and I will assign you to groups this week. We have one position available for the featured duet with Sergei. Please sign up for this role if interested in auditioning."

The ladies next to me giggled and glanced over at the handsome ballerino across the room. They each got up to sign up for the duet audition. I walked away without signing up. I was perfectly content to be part of a group number, just like I had been for every season.

Sergei looked at me intently.

I don't need his approval. I was determined not to let him intimidate me again.

"Emmett?" Camilla called for me as I was about to leave.

"Yes," I said.

"Why didn't you sign up for the duet?"

I stared at it for a moment, "I don't think I'm ready for that."

"That's the point of the audition," she said and added my name to the list.

* * *

After five other dancers had gone up and performed, it was my turn. My stomach was doing flips.

Why am I doing this?

Despite my internal protest I still pushed myself to do it.

I need to do this.

I had convinced myself that just auditioning was the next step I needed to take. I didn't care if I got the part or not but maybe this would give me the courage to try for other big roles in the company.

"Hello again," Sergei said with a smile as I approached him. He offered me a water bottle.

"Thanks," I said, taking a drink.

"Do you still stay after practice? You used to be the last to leave every night."

"Yeah," I said sheepishly.

He opened his mouth to say something but was interrupted by Camilla, "Let's begin!"

The beat pulsed through the studio as we circled each other, eyes locked. I moved forward and he stepped back, maintaining the distance between us.

On the beat change, I turned my back to him and he moved his arm around my waist, pulling me into him. His torso pressed against my back and the heat of his body met my chest. His free hand brushed against mine and gently intertwined our fingers.

"Are you always this timid," he teased, "or is it because of me?"

I spun from his hold, my shaking fingers pressed against his chest. His heart pounded against my palms.

His hands came to the small of my back as I leaned into a low dip. He swung me down even lower, then back up to face him.

"Maybe I was just intimidated by your…" I answered sharply, catching my breath.

He scoffed, "—by what, my old leopard print tights?"

"No," I responded, remembering those grotesque tights. "You intimidated me. You still intimidate me. Your skills, your looks, everything… but most of all you were always watching me. I could never relax."

"I never missed a chance to see you perform," he said and glided me around the dance space.

"Why? Were you sizing up your competition? Or trying to psych me out?"

He laughed, "Absolutely not!"

I spun back into him, my back was pressed to his chest again. He brought in our extended arms so that they wrapped around my chest.

"Then why were you always watching me?"

He whispered in my ear, "How could I avert my gaze from such a show?"

I lost my footing and fumbled the arabesque lift but Sergei smoothly caught me, flowing me into a twist just as the music ended.

"Are you all right?" he asked as Camilla thanked us.

I nodded, "Yes," His green eyes stared intently into mine. "I should sit back down, give the other dancers a try."

"Right," he said, "the other dancers."

He walked up to Camilla and spoke in her ear, then he left the room.

Camilla said, "We won't be seeing the rest of the auditions. We have our duo."

* * *

As I headed to practice, I overheard Bethany speak to James and Samantha, "Who does he think he is? He never tries out for anything and now all of the sudden he gets the part?"

"I didn't even get to audition!" Samantha added, stretching on the barre.

"Did you see the way Emmett fumbled the arabesque lift? Complete amateur," James said.

My chest felt heavy and the back of my eyes burned as I tried to fight back a rush of tears. I punched the metal door and pain seared through my hand. They stared at me in awkward silence before I ran down the hall.

Sergei was waiting for me in the other studio. He spun around when he heard me enter and throw my bag to the ground.

"What happened to you?"

"It's nothing," I snapped, holding my hand.

"Emmett, please, tell me what happened." He stepped towards me and took my injured hand. "Ouch. Are you okay?"

I moved away. "Let's just practice, okay?"

I switched on the music and jumped on the beat. Anger flooded my veins, and I pushed myself harder than ever. Tears started to fill my eyes and the room started to blur. I had to be perfect—I would be perfect.

"Emmett!" Sergei cried, "Emmett stop!"

"I have to do this," I said. I ran through the final sequence: the spin that leads into the arabesque lift. But it wasn't perfect. I pushed harder, spinning faster until my I collapsed onto the floor, twisting my ankle.

Sergei ran to my side and helped me up to the barre. I would be fine in a few hours.

"That's quite the routine," Bethany's voice called from the door. "I can't wait to see it at the Showcase next Friday."

Sergei's eyes narrowed. She stopped laughing and left.

He let out a deep sigh. He softened his gaze and turned it to me. Before I could respond, he had wrapped me in his arms. I reached around and clung to him while I cried into his tank top.

"Come on," he whispered, "I'm taking you home."

* * *

My studio apartment wasn't anything special, but it was homey with a small kitchen and an even smaller living room—just enough space for me and my loft-style bed.

"Welcome to my humble abode," I said, my voice exhausted as I tossed my keys into the bowl on the kitchen counter. I dropped into my loveseat.

"It's lovely," Sergei said. He pulled an ice pack out of the freezer.

"Promise me something?"

"What?" I looked down at him.

His hand placed the ice pack against my ankle.

"Forget what they said; they're only bitter." Our eyes locked. "Camilla trusted me to pick the right partner, and I did."

"But why? Bethany is a much better dancer than me, and you know it."

He looked out the window. The sunset outside cast a fiery glow over his face. "The right partner isn't the one with the best form or who knows the most advanced moves. A duet is about the connection between two souls."

He paused and took my hand. "I've never danced with Bethany, but watching you practice, we've completed a thousand duets in my mind."

"Yeah, but am I good enough to share the stage with you?"

"You see that sunset?" He gestured to the window. I looked outside. The bright neon lights illuminated the night sky in a dazzling array of colors. "When I hear music, I see colors; when I see you dance, I feel the colors move within you. I wish you could see it too because it's beautiful."

* * *

I found Sergei backstage, dressed in form-fitting alabaster shorts like me. He watched Bethany perform her solo to an adoring crowd.

"She's got talent," I remarked.

"Talent isn't everything. She has no heart." We met eyes for a moment, then Bethany's number ended.

"Great performance," Sergei said as Bethany passed.

She smirked. "I bet you regret not asking me to be your partner now."

He looked into my eyes, "I found the perfect partner."

My heart skipped a beat as Camilla's voice boomed across the stage, "Now please put your hands together for our next performers. Sergei Alekseyev and Emmett Price!"

A series of string instruments pulsated through the air, propelling us forward. Sergei grabbed my hand and glided me across the stage. For two and half minutes, I ceased being Emmett. Instead, I became one of the two souls of the dance, intertwined with Sergei. When he moved, I reacted. When I inhaled, he exhaled. All this time I was afraid to share the stage with him. But this felt right. When I dance with him I forget everyone else. I only see him and I forget why I was so afraid.

The final movement came too soon. I spun into his body, and he lifted me into the air. He twirled as I flew and then it was over. When my feet found the floor, his arms wrapped around me. I looked into his glittering eyes. I couldn't help but smile at him with delight. The curtain dropped as I kissed him to the sound of rapturous applause.

Quenched

September Roberts

Content Warning: Sexually Explicit

Twenty years. That's how long Veronica had waited for him.

She pulled her phone out of her back pocket for what must've been the hundredth time. Still nothing.

What did she expect? That he would call? Did he even know her number? After so long, would he even remember their pact? It was all she could think about, but that didn't mean he did.

"Anything?" Stephanie asked.

Veronica shook her head. "I'll give him until midnight." She sighed and checked the clock. "It's ridiculous, I know."

"It's romantic, not ridiculous." Steph hip-checked her and smiled. "Maybe you should cancel your class and go find him. I still can't understand why you wanted to teach on your birthday. You should be out there, sweeping him off his feet. That would be swoony."

"No. When we broke up, he said he would come find me in twenty years. On my birthday. That's what he promised."

Veronica fingered the pendant hanging around her neck as she always did when she thought of him, which was often. A few days ago, she'd doodled on her hand while waiting for customers, connecting the freckles, starting to spell his name. The faint *G* of ink still showed at the base of her thumb. Six years ago, she had made a pendant matching that *G* and hadn't taken it off.

Two women came into the shop. "We're here for the ring making class."

"You're in the right place," Veronica said with a smile, pushing all thoughts of him out of her head. "Why don't you head back into the classroom and get situated? We'll begin in a few minutes." She pointed to the corner where all the supplies were set out.

"Um, V? Can you come up here, please?" Steph called from the register.

With several sterling silver wires in her hand, Veronica made her way out of the classroom. Her breath hitched as she took in the sight of the tall man chatting with Stephanie. There's no way those broad shoulders and that fine ass could belong to anyone else. Gabe had actually remembered.

* * *

A soft, metal tinkling sound drew Gabe's attention. Veronica stood there, a delicious pink flush spread across her chest and neck. She looked even better than he remembered. He took a second to take her in, from the full curve of her hips to the bit of freckled skin exposed between her breasts. How many times had he undressed her and kissed along that delicate collarbone? Why had he taken her for granted? How long had he been staring at her? Embarrassment heated his cheeks as he picked up the strips of metal and tried to hand them to her. "Here you go."

"This customer was wondering if you had room in your class tonight," the woman behind the counter said, speaking to Veronica. "I wanted to check before I process his payment."

"Payment?" Veronica repeated, her eyes never leaving his.

"For your class?" the woman said with a laugh.

"Right." Veronica blinked and forced a smile with those beautiful lips. "Yes, I have room for one more." She swallowed hard and the blush spread across her cheeks. "Thanks for checking, Steph. Come on back when you're done, Gabe."

Veronica didn't seem happy to see him but what had he expected? That he'd just show up and say, "Surprise! It's me, the idiot who dumped you twenty years ago. Ready for another go?" She would never forgive him. This was a terrible idea.

"Sign here, then head back to the classroom," the woman said, pulling him out of his thoughts.

It was too late to leave now, so he nodded and followed the direction of her finger where two other women were already wearing safety glasses and listening attentively to what Veronica was telling them.

Without preamble, she handed him a piece of paper and continued talking. He signed his name at the bottom and handed it back to her.

"That's a safety waiver. You should read it. Know what you're getting yourself into." Veronica stared at him, a frown creasing her forehead.

"I know what I'm getting into," he said, hoping she understood he wasn't talking about the class. The last time he'd seen her, he'd been a stupid young guy with no plan for the future. She, on the other hand, had a grand future planned. If he'd been smart enough to hold onto her, his life would've been very different.

"Okay," she said as her frown deepened. "Put these on." She handed him a pair of safety glasses and that's when he saw the *G* drawn onto her skin. Heat burned through his chest as the memory surfaced. One night in bed, he'd found every letter of his name in the constellation of freckles covering her body. Foreplay always included claiming each one with his mouth.

He ran his thumb over her skin and her eyes met his. What was that? Desire? A shiver went through him. Maybe this hadn't been such a bad idea after all. As she pulled away, his fingers trailed along hers. A thrill of happiness zinged through him when he noticed she didn't wear a wedding ring.

Veronica cleared her throat. "Tonight, we're going to make a simple, silver ring." She kept her eyes focused on the other two students. "I'm here to guide you, but I want you to do the work. Learn what it feels like to sand, shape, and heat it. But first, you have to find the right size." With that, she produced a container of blue plastic bands and dumped them into a pile in the middle of the table. "It should be snug, but not too hard to get off."

The women across the table from him reached into the heap of plastic and chatted quietly amongst themselves, leaving Veronica's attention on him.

"What finger should I use?" he asked as he spread his hands out on the table and couldn't help but smile when she licked her lips.

"Um, you could make a thumb ring." She played with the delicate silver band around her own thumb.

"My knuckles are big, so it might be tricky to get off." As he spoke, her breathing sped up and she absentmindedly started playing with her necklace. A little silver *G* glinted between her breasts. It was the same size and shape as the *G* on her hand. He grinned. "Is that a *G*? My *G*?"

* * *

Veronica tried to clear her mind, but her proximity to Gabe made it nearly impossible. All she had to do was focus on teaching and stop staring at his mouth. And his hands. *Oh god, those talented hands.* She tucked her necklace away and stepped backward, bumping into the table with her tools, knocking some of them over.

"Are you okay?" Gabe asked, leaning toward her.

"Yes." *No.* How would she ever be okay again? He was right there, staring at her with that smile on his lips. She remembered those lips all over her body. *Stop it.* "Does everyone have their ring size picked out?"

The two women nodded in unison, but Gabe scrambled to find one, which he shoved onto his thumb and promptly grimaced.

"I think it's too small." Panic filled his eyes as he tugged at it. "It won't come off."

Veronica gave him a reassuring smile. "Don't worry, I have a trick that should work. Ladies, I want you to pick the kind of wire you want to use while I help him." She fanned out the stack, which all varied in width.

"Let's go to the utility sink," she said to Gabe, leading him to the other side of the room. "Soap should work."

Gabe followed her and thrust his hand out toward her when they reached the sink. "Thanks for helping me."

"Sure." She pumped some hand soap into her palm and coated his thumb generously, twisting and massaging the slippery liquid all over his digit. He closed his eyes and groaned. It was the same noise he used to make when she wrapped her hand around… something else. Her cheeks heated and she stilled her hands. He opened his eyes slowly, looking first at where they were touching, and then to her face. "Sorry," she said, but she didn't pull away from him.

"You have nothing to apologize for. I—"

"What do we do now?" one of the women called out from the classroom.

"Hang on, I'm coming," Veronica said.

"*Veronica*." Her name came out as a plaintive whisper.

"We can't. Not here. Not now."

With a quick tug, she pulled the ring smoothly off his big knuckle. "Maybe you should pick the next size up."

"Whatever you say." After he rinsed and dried his hands, they rejoined the rest of the class.

Thankfully, talking about her work seemed to break the spell between her and Gabe, and everything became easy again. He was just another student in her class. The only thing that mattered was helping them make rings.

* * *

Gabe did exactly what he was told, and his ring still looked horrible. He held the lumpy thing in his palm and scowled at it. She had made it look so easy.

"What's wrong?" Veronica asked.

"It looks awful."

"No, it doesn't. I told you it wouldn't be perfect. You can fix it later." She patted his arm in a way that was probably meant to be reassuring, but it only sparked his desire. She plucked the ring out of his hand, dropped it into a bowl with the other three, and addressed the class, "This pickling solution will clean off the oxidized metal from the solder. It will take a few minutes. Feel free to roam through the store, use the bathroom, or grab a snack. See you back here in ten minutes." She set a timer on her phone and turned her back to him while she organized her tools. The other two students disappeared into the store, leaving them alone again.

He stepped up behind her, wishing he could wrap his arms around her. "It's good to see you again, Veronica."

She turned and looked up at him. "It's good to see you too." Her voice was barely audible. "How did you find me?" She sighed. "I didn't mean for that to sound accusatory. It's just that a lot has happened in twenty years and I'm not where I was then."

"Did you ever get married?" he blurted out, unable to wait another minute before finding out.

"I did, but it didn't stick." She frowned.

"I'm sorry," he said, and he meant it.

"Are you?" Her frown deepened and she stepped away from him.

That's what she had wanted from him. Marriage, kids, and a house in the suburbs. It had scared the shit out of him. "I know how much you wanted that. What happened?"

She dropped her shoulders a little. "We were happy for a while, and then we weren't. How about you?"

"No one ever stuck to me, either. Are you seeing anyone?"

"No. You?"

He shook his head and closed the gap between them and took her hand in his, another pulse of pleasure shot through him. "I thought I imagined this."

"What?" She blinked slowly. *Could she sense it too?*

"The feeling I get when I touch you." It was the same all-consuming need he felt when they first met. The need to touch her. Taste her. Be inside her.

"No one has ever made me feel the way you do." Her soft words made his heart race faster.

"Can I kiss you?"

Veronica nodded and leaned toward him, her breath coming fast and shallow. Gabe lowered his face until their lips were almost touching. That's when her alarm rang.

* * *

"Shit," Veronica muttered under her breath as she fumbled to pull her phone out of her back pocket to silence the alarm. *How had it already been ten minutes?* Time flies when you're trying to make out with your old boyfriend. With a bright smile plastered on her heated face, she directed her students to their seats so they could get back to work. "Now we quench our rings again," she said as she dropped the rings into water. After her near kiss with Gabe, she wished she had a bowl big enough to quench her entire body. Maybe that would put out the fires he stirred in her. Or, maybe the only way to get him out of her system was to take him home and—*stop it.*

She had to focus on work, her sanity depended on it. So that's what she did. She distributed their rings and the tools they would need, then she slid her ring onto the tapered mandrel and tapped the ring gently with a rawhide mallet to demonstrate the technique.

"Take your time. This is a slow process." She started with the women first, giving them pointers then leaving them to their work, their backs to Gabe. When she turned her attention to him, she noticed it was hard to think about work when he spoke.

"How am I doing?" Gabe asked, turning his body toward her, holding the ring and mandrel up for her inspection.

"Uh-huh." She wrapped her hand around his. His skin was so warm and smooth.

"Veronica?" A smile played on his lips.

"Uh-huh?" She tore her gaze away from his mouth and met his eyes. "What did you say?"

"How am I doing?"

She looked down at their hands and the ring he'd been working on. "Oh, that. Fine. What are you doing after class?" she whispered. There were all sorts of things she wanted to do to him and none of them involved a mandrel or classroom. She clearly needed to take him home to get him out of her system.

"I planned to apologize for making the biggest mistake of my life."

That stopped her sexy-time thoughts. "To me?"

"Of course, to you." He stroked her arm and heat went through her. "I owe you that. And more."

The way he said *more* made her brain mushy. What did it mean? More talking? More kissing? More touching? She hoped it was the latter. "Uh-huh."

Gabe laughed. "How much longer is class?" She shook her head, trying to clear the fog in her brain, and stepped away from him. "An hour." She could wait an hour, couldn't she?

He groaned, the sound filled with need and frustration.

Knowing he was just as wound up as her made her ridiculously happy. "Aren't you having a good time?"

"My idea of a good time involves a lot less clothes," he whispered.

She couldn't stifle the gasp that came out of her mouth, which she quickly covered with a cough. If she could survive the next hour, it would be a miracle.

* * *

At the end of class, Gabe wrapped his arm around Veronica's waist and followed her out of the building and down the sidewalk. When they turned the corner at the end of the building, Veronica faced him and crushed her lips against his. Surprise quickly gave way to the need he'd kept in check all night. He caressed the sides of her face as Veronica deepened the kiss. He leaned back against the rough brick wall to steady them. When she rubbed her breasts against his chest, he groaned and pulled away, hitting his head into the wall. "I missed you."

Veronica licked her swollen lips and nodded. "So much."

"I'm so sorry. I—" Before he could go on, she kissed him again, this time, pushing her tongue into his mouth. She ran her hands down his waist and cupped his ass, pulling their bodies together. When his erection pressed against her heat, he almost came right then and there. "We need to go somewhere."

"My place. I live two blocks away."

Hand in hand, they walked briskly to the new apartment complex downtown. Her fingers shook as she unlocked the outer door. "Follow me," she said as she started up a flight of stairs. With her perfect round ass nearly level with his face, he gladly followed. At the top of the stairs, she stopped in front of a door and again fumbled with her keys. He came up behind her and she leaned back into him, pressing her body firmly against his.

"Oh shit, you feel so good." Veronica's voice was breathy and her body went slack as he wrapped an arm around her and rolled his hips. She moaned when he kissed the nape of her neck. "We should go inside."

"Mm-hm." He definitely wanted inside. As soon as she got the door open, she flipped on a light, pulled him in, and tugged on the hem of his shirt. He helped her ease it over his head and fumbled to kick the door closed behind them.

She sighed and ran her fingers across his chest. He shivered when she traced the same path with her mouth, trailing kisses along his sensitive skin. "Veronica."

"Gabriel." She looked up at him, her strawberry gold hair framing her beautiful face.

The sound of his full name on her lips was enough to trigger a flood of memories, and he couldn't wait to find all seven letters on her body.

She guided him into the small living area and pushed him onto the couch, straddling his lap. He picked up her hand and kissed the patch of freckles that formed the *G*, tracing the shape with the tip of his tongue. "Mine." The *A* freckle formation was hidden by her shirt. "Can I take your shirt off?"

Veronica hesitated. "My body has changed a lot in twenty years."

"I've always loved your body. I'd like a chance to get to know this new one, too."

She smiled gently and nodded, lifting her shirt and dropping it onto the floor.

"You're beautiful." She was softer and fuller than before and the sight of her on top of him in this state of undress made him impossibly hard. "I love your new body." He ran his hands over her soft skin, enjoying every inch of her.

She smiled shyly. "I have more freckles, but don't worry, your *A* is still right here." She pointed to the spot near her left breast, just above the cup of her bra, which he traced with his lips and tongue.

"Mine."

She moaned and rocked down into him. "This feels better than I remember."

He lifted his hips to meet her and she moved again and again, rubbing against his length, a flush spreading over her body, tinging her freckle formations a lovely pink. She held her breath and squeezed her eyes shut as her orgasm took over, making her body vibrate against his. He couldn't stop himself from following. The thunderous sound of his blood pulsing in his ears muffled everything, including the sound of someone opening the front door.

"My study group ended early tonight, so I thought I'd surprise you with a holy shit." The man's voice cut off abruptly as his eyes met Gabe's.

* * *

Veronica jumped at the sound of Henry's voice and the loss of contact between her and Gabe sent a pang of desperation through her.

"What the hell?" Henry said, his voice coming from the kitchen, where he was no doubt hiding.

"It's not what it looks like." Veronica laughed. It was exactly what it looked like. She slid off the couch and tugged her shirt over her head. Once her face popped out the top, she looked at Gabe, who still sat on the couch, a dark spot spreading across his crotch. Well, that confirmed her suspicion of just how hot their make out session had been.

He clenched his jaw and when he spoke, his words came out low and threatening. "Who the hell is he?"

Henry scoffed. "Who the hell are you? I live here."

Hurt slashed through Gabe's features. As if she had cheated on him. No, not on him. With him. Before she could clear up this mess, Henry opened his mouth.

"Jesus, Mom. Why didn't you text to let me know? Are you dressed?"

"Mom?" Gabe frowned.

"Yes," she said, answering both of them. Henry poked his head out of the kitchen just in time for introductions. "Henry, this is Gabe. Gabe, this is my son, Henry."

"You have a son?" His mouth hung open.

"Wait, the Gabe?" Henry came into full view, a small birthday cake in his hands, realization dawning on his face. "I completely forgot about tonight. I guess he found you, huh?"

Gabe frowned and stood up. Veronica lunged to pick up Gabe's shirt and pressed it against the fly of his jeans.

"He found me."

Henry held the cake in one hand and offered his other to Gabe, but pulled it back almost immediately. "On second thought, I don't know where those hands have been."

"Honey," Veronica scolded.

"Don't pretend you're innocent. Your shirt is on backward, by the way." Henry smirked.

Gabe stared at Henry, narrowing his eyes. "He's named after your dad, isn't he? He looks just like him. It's uncanny."

"You knew my grandpa?"

Gabe nodded and a smile softened the edges of his mouth. "It's like being a teenager again and getting caught by your dad. Talk about déjà vu."

"No one is supposed to catch anyone doing anything. This is why we have a system," Henry said.

"Our system has been one-sided until now. I forgot, okay?" Heat spread across her cheeks.

Henry sighed. "I guess I'll let it slide, but know you've scarred me for life."

"Oh, please." Veronica huffed. "I'm sure you and your therapist are going to have a hay day with this."

A smile broke across Henry's face. "True. Now, if you'll excuse me, I'm going to David's place for the night. Maybe we could all get together for dinner this weekend, as long as you promise to wear all your clothes." Veronica scowled at him.

"Happy birthday, Mom." He leaned toward her and kissed her cheek, then whispered, "I can totally see the appeal. Have fun tonight."

"Henry!" She tried to swat him, but he darted away.

"Save me a piece of cake?"

"Would you leave already?" Veronica laughed and pushed him out the door. She turned around slowly, biting her bottom lip. "That is not how I wanted you to meet Henry."

***

"You have a son," Gabe repeated, still unable to process everything that had just happened.

"I do. Sorry I forgot to text him. We have a system. When he has someone over, he lets me know so I can give them privacy. I've never had to use the system before."

"He's so like you." Relief and grief battled inside him. He was relieved she had gotten what she wanted most, a family, but mourned the fact that he hadn't been a part of it.

"He and I have always been close. It made Brad jealous, I think."

"Your ex?"

Veronica nodded and tears welled in her eyes. "Brad wanted a family too, so we got married a few months after we met and started trying to get pregnant. I thought he was the perfect man." She shook her head and squeezed her eyes shut, forcing tears down her cheeks. "He left when Henry came out. He was ten. I always knew, and I thought Brad did too." She paused and searched his eyes, probably to gauge his reaction. "He said the most hurtful things."

Gabe gathered her into his arms and hugged her. "I think Henry is wonderful. Your dad would've loved him."

She wiped at her cheeks and smiled. "That's what I always say."

"Why didn't you tell me about him?"

Veronica shrugged then put her hands on his chest. "I didn't want him to get hurt again. Plus, it seemed too soon. Like it was too much all at once."

"I'll never hurt him," Gabe said and she relaxed in his arms. "And if I've learned anything from my past mistakes, it's that there's no such thing as too much at once. I want it all when it comes to you." He stroked the soft skin of her back through the V-neck opening of her backward shirt.

"And I want to give it to you. I always have."

They kissed again, their lips moving slowly at first, but when her hands moved down his stomach, he growled and bit at her playfully.

"We made a mess earlier," Veronica said. She traced the waistband of his jeans. "Can I help you out of these?"

Gabe frowned and glanced at the front door. "Can we go to your room?"

"Yes, please."

He followed her down the hall into the small bedroom and sighed when she closed and locked the door.

"Now can I finish undressing you?" she asked.

"Only if I can return the favor."

"Deal." With that, she unbuttoned his jeans and pushed them onto the floor, her hot gaze lingering at the tent in his sticky boxers.

He kicked his shoes and socks off with his jeans. "Where were we? Oh yes, I remember." He tugged her shirt off and kissed across her collarbone and down to her left breast. Next, he sank to his knees and unbuttoned her pants, tracing the *B* at her hip with his tongue. "Mine."

She dug her fingers into his hair and moaned. He loved that sound and wanted to hear it again, so he lowered her onto the bed and undressed her slowly until she was only wearing her bra and panties. Positioned between her legs, he wanted to sink into her soft, pliable body. It took every ounce of restraint to stay focused. He lifted her right leg up to his face and found the *R* in the cluster of freckles, which he kissed and licked. "Mine."

Veronica giggled when he claimed the *I* on her left knee. That had always been a ticklish spot. The *E* on her inner thigh made her moan. "Mine." Her breath came quick and ragged. He traced her slit through her damp panties with his thumb, outlining the *L* buried in soft, fiery curls. "Mine?"

"Yours," she hissed, lifting off the bed, offering herself to him.

Tugging the scrap of fabric out of the way, he slid his tongue inside her. His hips jerked against the bed as the taste of her promised the pleasure to come. He sucked and nipped, pushing her over the edge of release within seconds.

"You remember what I like." Her words were shaky.

"How could I forget?" he said, smiling above her.

"I remember, too," she said, rolling them until she was straddling him. She reached across to her nightstand and pulled out a brand-new box of condoms. She tore one off the strip and wiggled down his body. Within a few seconds, she had his boxers off and his cock in her hand.

She remembered everything he liked, down to the way she rolled the condom over him. Propping herself up on one elbow, she pushed her panties off her legs and kicked them to the floor.

"You are the sexiest woman I've ever seen."

Words failed him when she positioned the head of his dick against her wet heat. She smiled and unclasped her bra, cupping her full breasts and playing with her nipples. Her mouth fell open when she sank down on him, taking him in slowly. "Mine," she whispered.

"Yours," he agreed. "I love you, Veronica."

"I love you, Gabe. Always have, always will."

Author Bios

Elizabeth Suggs
Elizabeth Suggs is the president of the LUW Romance
Chapter, co-owner of the indie publisher Collective
Tales Publishing, owner of Editing Mee, and is the
author of a growing number of published stories, two
of which were in a podcast and poetry journal. She is a
book reviewer (EditingMee.com) and popular booksta-
gramer and cosplayer (@ElizabethSuggsAuthor). When
she's not writing or reading, she's playing video/board
games or making cookies.

Virginia Babcock
Virginia Babcock is the vice-president of the LUW Romance Chapter. She has always loved romantic fiction,
and now writes her own stories of love and life in the
real world. Virginia lives in Missouri where she works

full-time when she's not writing books. The rest of her free time is spent with her husband and cat.

Stacy Wrytes
Stacy Wrytes was born a California girl but spent most of her youth in Utah. She loves the seasonal changes that the mountains provide but hates the snow. She makes regular pilgrimages back to the land of her birth to feed her Disney addiction. Stacy loves animals and will cross the street just to say hi to a dog. She would absolutely own several if not for her allergies. Her regular bouts of insomnia inspire her writing, as she has nothing better to do at 2am when her mind won't shut off.

Debra Birdwell Winkler
Debra Birdwell Winkler's writing career started when she won a poetry award in 5th grade, and she has been writing ever since. When she retired, she was finally able to concentrate on her writing, which has become her focus, her job, her joy. Every story of hers is related to a piece of music. The title, "Never in a Million Years," is taken from the chorus of a 1958 song called, "Oh-Oh I'm Falling in Love Again," by Jimmie Rodgers.

Jonathan Reddoch
Jonathan Reddoch is co-owner of Collective Tales Publishing. He is a father, writer, editor, and publisher. He writes sci-fi, fantasy, romance, and especially horror. He has been working on his enormous sci-fi novel for over a decade and would like to finish it in this lifetime if possible. Find him on Instagram: @Allusions_of_Grandeur_

September Roberts
September Roberts writes romance erotica in a variety of genres. Whether it's paranormal, new adult, or contemporary, you'll always get the happy ever after you've come to

expect from her. She creates true-to-life romance, smart characters, strong heroines, intimate scenes, and plenty of humor.

Bryan Young

Bryan Young (he/they) works across many different media. His work as a writer and producer has been called "filmmaking gold" by *The New York Times*. He's also published comic books with Slave Labor Graphics and Image Comics. He's been a regular contributor for the *Huffington Post*, *StarWars.com*, *Star Wars Insider magazine*, *SYFY*, */Film*, and was the founder and editor in chief of the geek news and review site *Big Shiny Robot!* He co-authored *Robotech: The Macross Saga RPG* in 2019 and in 2020 he wrote a novel in the BattleTech Universe called *Honor's Gauntlet*. He currently serves as the president of the League of Utah Writers. Follow him on Twitter @swankmotron.

Sara Wetmore

Sara Wetmore is an award-winning author who studied creative writing at Lindenwood University, where she earned her MFA. She is the author of *The Golden Girl* and *Brush Strokes*. When she's not writing, you can catch her traveling the world with her husband or playing with her two cats.

Sarah Alva

Sarah Alva lives in Salt Lake City, UT but calls Arizona home. In college, she once told a creative writing workshop she wanted to grow up to be a stay-in-bed mom. She's almost living that dream with two little boys, but they don't like naps as much as she does. When Sarah isn't reading, writing, or mom-ing, she enjoys painting her nails, watching trash TV, and listening to NPR. She is on social media as @authorsaraha.

Liz Christensen
Liz Christensen is the host and producer of the "In the Telling" podcast and the "She Made Me Do It" web series. She is a writer, director, choreographer, film actress, audiobook narrator, and hiker. The youngest of 13 children in a blended family, she is the mother of two teenagers and married to the love of her life. Her best scars come from being an obstacle course racer. She graduated magna cum laude from the University of Utah with a BFA and is pursuing her masters of arts in English teaching. You can find more of her work at lizzylizzyliz.com.

Austin Slade Perry
As a child, Austin Slade Perry was always told he had an overactive imagination. When he grew up, that imagination transformed into storytelling and his passion for writing. He also finds joy in other creative outlets, such as drawing, designing, cooking, and supporting his friends with their artistic passions.

Join Our Group!

The LUW Romance Chapter is a group open to everyone who dabbles in romance! Check out our meetings and future anthologies at www.LUWRomance.Wordpress.com